"Dinner with you and Lily?"

"Yes, she can be our chaperone."

"Are we in need of a chaperone?"

Too quick. Too feisty. Too full-on, Sophia!

Something flashed in Jack's gaze, something akin to the heat streaking right to her toes as she realized she couldn't take back her reckless words and knew she didn't want to, either.

"So, what do you say?"

She didn't know whether she should be disappointed or relieved that he didn't answer her question. Not directly at any rate.

But what should she say?

No, because the chemistry between us is scaring the life out of me.

No, because I'm messed up and in no place for whatever this is.

No, because...just because.

"You know, I really am starting to question my charm."

His grin, filled with the very charm she'd brought into question, seared away any intention of saying no.

And what was there to say no to when she thought about it rationally?

She enjoyed his company. She'd enjoyed Lily's company that afternoon. Would it really be so bad to go to dinner?

Dear Reader,

I can't quite believe I'm sending this little letter to you from the pages of my debut Harlequin Romance novel. I've lived and breathed Mills & Boon for too many years to count, as a reader and as an aspiring writer, and now a published one, too. It truly is an honor to bring this tale to you. The idea that you will spend your precious time getting swept up in a world I've created is incredibly humbling and heartwarming. It's a feeling that will never get old and I thank you from the bottom of my heart.

As for the tale itself, it's a story of loss, of losing loved ones and the guilt that can consume us. But it's also a story of hope, of what comes next. It's a story of healing, of learning to trust and let go, to love and be loved in return. It's about the bond between family, lovers and friends, the many facets of love, and I hope you find the same joy in reading it as I did writing it.

Love,

Rachael x

Tempted by the Tycoon's Proposal

—

Rachael Stewart

H HARLEQUIN

Romance

HARLEQUIN®

Romance™

Recycling programs
for this product may
not exist in your area.

ISBN-13: 978-1-335-56683-6

Tempted by the Tycoon's Proposal

Copyright © 2021 by Rachael Stewart

All rights reserved. No part of this book may be used or reproduced in
any manner whatsoever without written permission except in the case of
brief quotations embodied in critical articles and reviews.

This is a work of fiction. Names, characters, places and incidents
are either the product of the author's imagination or are used fictitiously.
Any resemblance to actual persons, living or dead, businesses,
companies, events or locales is entirely coincidental.

This edition published by arrangement with Harlequin Books S.A.

For questions and comments about the quality of this book,
please contact us at CustomerService@Harlequin.com.

Harlequin Enterprises ULC
22 Adelaide St. West, 40th Floor
Toronto, Ontario M5H 4E3, Canada
www.Harlequin.com

Printed in U.S.A.

Rachael Stewart adores conjuring up stories, from heartwarmingly romantic to wildly erotic. She's been writing since she could put pen to paper—as the stacks of scrawled-on pages in her loft will attest to. A Welsh lass at heart, she now lives in Yorkshire, with her very own hero and three awesome kids—and if she's not tapping out a story, she's wrapped up in one or enjoying the great outdoors. Reach her on Facebook, Twitter (@rach_b52) or at rachaelstewartauthor.com.

Books by Rachael Stewart

Tempted by the Tycoon's Proposal
is **Rachael Stewart**'s debut title for
Harlequin Romance.

Look out for more books coming soon!

In the meantime, why not try Rachael Stewart's
Harlequin DARE titles:

Mr. One-Night Stand
Mr. Temptation
Naughty or Nice
Getting Dirty
Losing Control
Unwrapping the Best Man

Visit the Author Profile page at Harlequin.com.

For my editor, Carly,

For believing in me when I struggled to believe in myself and making this another dream come true, this one is for you!

Rachael x

CHAPTER ONE

'Soph, we have a situation.'

Normally those words from her extremely capable assistant hotel manager would have had Sophia Lambert on edge, but not today. Today, she needed the distraction. In fact, she'd take a month of situations just to get through January and keep the past at bay.

Taking a breath, she turned from her computer screen to give Andrew a smile and felt it freeze midway.

Whatever it was, it wasn't good. Andrew was unflappable and yet his age-old wrinkles were creased tight, his warm eyes bright with concern.

Maybe this would be a distraction too far...

'What is it?'

'The McGregor child has gone missing.'

'Missing?' Her semi-smile became a frown. The McGregors were staying in the penthouse suite, one of the most luxurious suites London had to offer and as such rarely used. Only the richest of the rich could afford its extortionate nightly rate and the billionaire businessman McGregor was one such man.

A widower too. Not that Sophia knew this first-hand; the trusty grapevine of the hotel trade was responsible for that. His financial status and the tragic tale of a hit-and-run that took his wife three years ago, and almost took his child too, had spread far and wide thanks to the world's media. She could just imagine how fast news of his child being missing would spread…

'She came back with her nanny just after lunch and before they made it to her room…' He shrugged, the move stilted with unease. 'Poof—vanished.'

Sophia shook her head and pushed herself out of her seat. 'A little girl can hardly vanish.'

Although, if she was honest, she'd disappear if she was in the care of that particular woman. She hadn't had the pleasure of meeting the illustrious McGregor yet—he hadn't arrived—but she'd met his little miss of a daughter and the battle-axe caring for her.

She approached him in the doorway. 'We have twelve floors, one hundred and thirty rooms, cupboards, trolleys, luggage; if the girl wants to hide, she's in the right place. There's no need to think the worst.'

He scratched his brow. 'I hope so.'

'Come on.' She started off down the corridor

that led into the main foyer. 'Where have you tried?'

'The toilets, the public rooms downstairs, the lifts and stairwell.'

'Okay, who's on the search?'

'Everyone who's not needed out front. I even have the maids who were due to clock off hunting and Marie has taken Ms Archer back to the penthouse to calm her nerves.'

Marie was a good choice. Calm, efficient, matronly even, and a fabulous head housekeeper. 'Good.'

'But it's been half an hour; we'll have to call the police soon.'

'We'll find her.' Sophia paused to rest a hand on his shoulder. 'What about CCTV?'

He nodded. 'We've checked. She was last seen heading towards the conference room on the second floor.'

'And you've tried there?'

'Of course—no joy.'

'But there's no sign of her leaving the building?'

He shook his head. 'Absolutely none.'

'There we go; she has to be here somewhere. We just have to think like a child and we'll find her. I'm going to head up to the conference room; you carry on the search down here. Call me if you find her.'

'Will do.'

They branched off and Sophia took to the stairs.

She wasn't ready to worry yet. Things and people went missing in hotels every day and it was their job to see it resolved, to keep the guests happy. Which included Little Miss Trouble and her elusive father.

The conference room looked deserted, tables and chairs all stacked neatly to one side ready to be laid out for a company's belated Christmas function. One table had already been set up, a red cloth covering it, with flowers, glassware and napkins all arranged to the organisers' exacting standards. But no child.

She turned to leave and then something caught her eye. She looked back, eyes narrowing on the tablecloth. She could have sworn it had fluttered.

'Hello?' She took a tentative step towards it. Another flutter. Definite this time. 'Hello?'

This time she got a small giggle in response and her heart lifted. 'Is that you, Miss McGregor?'

'I don't have time for this, Connor. Why wasn't it on our radar?'

Jack scowled at the hotel doorman. It wasn't intentional—his mind was on the call—but it got the door opened promptly and he was off, striding across the foyer. He pressed the button to call the lift and threw his focus down the line, surveying the room with unseeing eyes.

'We hadn't even heard of them before today,'

Connor was saying. 'Apparently it's some new start-up that's done well enough to outbid us.'

Fantastic. This was all he needed. The plan had been to fly into London, stay for a week—two at most—get the takeover signed and get out again. He hated the city at the best of times. Too cold, too grey, too loaded with the past.

'Well, get digging. I want to know all there is by close of play t—'

'Er...excuse me, Mr McGregor.'

Jack frowned and turned towards the voice. A quick appraisal of the man's uniform and badge told him he was the assistant manager and he looked nervous, his hands wringing before him.

'Hang on, Connor... Yes?'

'I'm afraid, sir...' he bowed his head slightly '...we have a...situation.'

The guy had to be kidding. Was this really going to be his life today? Connor had used the exact same words not twenty minutes ago.

'What kind of situation?' He couldn't think for a second what it would be. Was his room not ready? Had there been a double booking? Nothing could be worse than Connor's unwelcome news. 'Well?'

The guy stopped wringing his hands and placed them behind his back, his chin lifting. 'It's your daughter... I'm afraid she's gone—'

His walkie-talkie sounded as Jack's stomach took a dive, and the manager jolted as he scrambled to pull the device out of the pocket of his hotel-issue blazer. 'Yes?'

Jack couldn't catch what was said over the blood ringing in his ears, his patience hanging by a thread. What the devil was going on? What *had* Lily done now?

The guy physically relaxed before him, his body deflating as he blew out a gust of air. 'That's great news. Thank you!'

He repocketed the device and smiled up at him. 'I'm very happy to report all is well.'

Jack just frowned. 'Excuse me?'

'Sorry, Jack,' Connor piped down the phone line, 'like I was saying—'

'Not you...*you*.' He glared at the manager, now flushing crimson.

'Pardon me, sir. It's just...it seems your daughter decided to play a little hide-and-seek with Ms Archer this afternoon. However, she has now been found and—'

He cursed, his head and heart racing with a multitude of what-ifs that didn't even matter now that she was found, but they existed anyway. 'How long was she missing?'

'Well... I... It was...' He started to wring his hands again. 'I'm not sure. Perhaps Ms Archer can explain. I'll take you to your daughter, shall I? She's with Ms Lambert, our hotel manager.'

Jack gave him a brusque nod. 'Connor, I'll call you back.' He cut the line and followed after the manager, who was already walking away faster than his advancing years would suggest possible.

Jack shook his head and pulled at his tie, easing it away from his neck as his skin prickled and perspired, the stress building in spite of her safety. This really was not his day. And as far as Lily's nanny-cum-tutor went, maybe it was time to find another—something Lily would no doubt appreciate.

But he paid her to look after Lily twenty-four-seven and in the last two weeks alone she had misplaced her a dozen times. He really was at his wits' end, let alone his nerves.

Finding another would take time—time he didn't have. What he really should be doing was explaining the dangers to his daughter, making her realise her safety was more important than whatever distraction she had sought out this time. And he could just imagine how much of that she would take on board. She was too much like her mother: free-spirited, impulsive, a sitting target for another hit-and-run or, heaven forbid, a kidnapper seeking a ridiculous ransom sum.

And how exactly did he tell his five-year-old daughter that her father's success made her a target? That for all he worked to ensure their financial stability and a quality of life that far exceeded anything he had ever known, she was to be caged by it too. Maybe it was high time he employed a security detail. He'd avoided it thus far, trying to retain some normality for his daughter, but he wasn't sure how many more of these incidents, these disappearing acts, he could take.

'They're just this way, Mr McGregor...' the manager said, ending Jack's troubled inner ramblings as he pushed open a door and gestured for him to enter.

He gave him a grim nod, being too strung-out to speak. And it wasn't this guy's fault his temper was frayed. It was all—

He didn't get to finish the thought. He was too surprised to do anything but gawp.

And he *never* gawped.

Before him was a festive table. A festive table with a pair of nude stilettos attached to dainty ankles and slender calves poking out beneath its deep red tablecloth.

What the devil?

Within minutes of meeting the little girl, Sophia found herself lying on her back beneath the beautifully laid table staring at its underside, while Miss McGregor flashed a torch at it.

'Isn't it pretty?' The little girl rolled the *r* as she waved her hand at the star constellation the torch projected.

'It is...and clever... Is this what you've been doing all this time? You know Ms Archer has been quite worried about you.'

The girl gave a dramatic frown, her eyes, dark

in the low light, now appeared both serious and disappointed at once. Here it came—the excuse. There always was one with children and Sophia had a sneaky suspicion she was going to be reeled in regardless.

'She never lets me look at the stars. She says it's a waste of my noggin.' She prodded her forehead with one forefinger as she stared Sophia down. 'That I should be learning my maths and reading.'

'Well, I'm sure Ms Archer just wants what's best for you.'

She looked back to the lit-up stars. 'I'm going to be an astronaut; I don't need maths…or the books she wants me to read.'

Sophia gave a soft laugh. 'Maths will certainly help you if that's what you want to be when you grow up.'

'Really?'

Really.

She sighed heavily, her bottom lip jutting out. 'Maybe I will try a little—'

'What on earth?' The heavy booming voice took over the girl's and her eyes widened as she switched off the torch.

'Uh-oh, Daddy's mad.'

Daddy's mad… Oh, no.

Sophia imagined the scene from Mr Mc-Gregor's eyes and felt the heat radiate out from her middle, her cheeks burning bright. All he would see were her calves and her shoes, like something out of *The Wizard of Oz*... Only her shoes weren't red; they were nude and attached to her. No witch, just a blushing hotel manager about to face the music.

Not that there was anything to be apologetic or embarrassed about. She'd found his daughter and really he ought to be grateful for that, not—

'Lily, come out here this minute.'

'I'm sorry,' the little girl whispered to Sophia, her hair a bobbing mass of dark ringlets as she clambered onto her knees and crawled out backward. She made it look so simple, almost graceful, and Sophia ought to do the same.

She really ought to.

Really, *really* ought to.

But there was something vulnerable about being caught lying on your back beneath a table, the oddity of the situation leaving her quite incapable of thinking straight.

'What do you think you're doing, running out on Ms Archer like that?'

Sophia couldn't make out the girl's response, just a short, sharp sniff. The next thing she knew, the tablecloth was being flicked up and the most dramatic pair of grey eyes speared her. 'Ms Lambert, I presume?'

She looked down her nose at him, literally, since she was still lying back on the floor and wishing the ground would swallow her up. Particularly as the eyes spearing her were far too attractive and far too hard all at once.

Get with it, Sophia.

She cleared her throat and rolled onto her knees, mimicking his daughter's method, only she was very much focused on tugging her dress as low as possible over her behind and doing her utmost to avoid not only his eye but his entire body.

Even in his crouched position he exuded a panther-like grace. All power, sinew and strength, in a dark suit complete with tie…and the effect he was having on her pulse really wasn't helping her focus on words. Words of any shape or form.

'It's a pleasure to meet you, Mr McGregor,' she said, finally standing and lifting her gaze, only to wish she'd kept it lowered. Yes, she knew he was a widower. Yes, she knew he was the father to a young daughter. Yes, she knew he had a reputation for being a bit of a looker. But for some reason she'd had him pegged as being older, his reputation stemming from money and power, not a seriously impressive frame and a face that belonged on the cover of a magazine.

His body too, she was sure—

She swallowed and cut the thought dead. It was entirely inappropriate and in no way helping her function in a manner befitting her professional role. He was a guest for goodness' sake, a very important guest, the kind she should be impressing, not… What exactly was she doing?

'Jack.' He offered his hand and she jumped a little.

Great. Now she just looked scared. And judging by the way his brow lifted and his lips—his very full and teasing lips—quirked he'd not missed her overreaction either. *Even better...*

'Sophia.' She forced a smile and quickly slotted her hand in his, but his eyes stayed locked with hers, their intensity making her feel exposed, as if he could read every debauched thought racing through her mind and her cheeks flushed all over again.

Another swallow, another breath and a shake of the hand. At least she hoped she'd shaken it because the warmth zinging along her fingers, through her wrist, her arm and settling somewhere around her tummy made it hard to focus on the actual giving of a handshake.

He didn't seem disturbed though; his eyes were sharp as they assessed her. For what she couldn't really tell, but she had a fair idea what a panther's prey felt like seconds before it pounced.

Maybe it was his unruly dark hair, the rich colour to his skin and the slant to his dramatic grey eyes that had her heading down the wild-cat route. Whatever the case, she was off on some weird tangent where professionalism continued to evade her.

'I like Sphea. Can she come for tea, Daddy?'

What? No! Sophia's laugh came out a strangled

mess, thankfully drowned out by a sudden bellow from the man before her. So the panther was capable of laughter. Fascinating. And distracting. Especially when she should be drawing a line under that right now. She did not socialise, fraternise or any other *ise* with the clientele.

'I think Sphea has far more important things to be taking care of...'

The way he mimicked his daughter's pronunciation of her name had her entire insides turning to mush and she opened her mouth to agree but nothing came out.

'Unless, of course, that is not the case?'

He turned to pin her with that far too astute gaze. 'Then you would be more than welcome this evening, as a thank you for finding my little runaway.'

Sophia looked from him to the little girl staring imploringly up at her, eyes the colour of her father's, and erupted in a nervous giggle which she abruptly quit as her eyes caught sight of Andrew in the open doorway. He was positively beaming, reading whatever he fancied into her crazed behaviour. *Great.*

She would sort that, just as soon as she turned down Mr McGregor's very kind and far too appealing offer. But how exactly could she turn down their most lucrative customer without causing offence?

Stick to work—something he'd understand...

* * *

What are you doing, Jack?

Looking down into the alluring blue gaze of Sophia Lambert, he really had no idea. She was the hotel manager, not some new friend his daughter had taken a shine to. He blamed the crazy suggestion entirely on Lily of course. If she hadn't put the idea out there, he certainly wouldn't have thought of it and he definitely wouldn't have found it as appealing as he did.

Hot off the back of the little display that had greeted him when he'd first entered the conference room, he wasn't so certain he was thinking with his brain either. Two slender calves, a pair of stilettos and the knowledge that the woman had got down to his daughter's level, no airs and graces, tugged at him even now.

Sophia blinked, and blinked again, her cheeks a delightful shade of pink as her eyes adjusted to some unknown thought and then she drew in a breath and crouched down to Lily's height.

His view was reduced to her auburn hair, knotted high, her escaped curls that brushed over the creamy skin at her nape and the dusting of freckles that disappeared into the high neck of her navy dress. He cleared his throat, surprised to find his mouth as dry as the Sahara.

'It's so kind of you to offer, Lily,' she said softly, 'but I'm afraid I need to work.'

'Now you sound like Daddy.'

He cringed inwardly as Sophia sent him a brief look. It wasn't how he wanted to be; it was how he had to be. You didn't get to run a billion-pound company taking it easy. You didn't get to provide a financially stable home without putting in the hours. Lily had so much more than he'd ever had, and his work saw to it she always would.

'Well, you see this big building—this hotel?' Lily nodded at her. 'If I don't work, then this place doesn't work. I make sure important guests like you are taken care of and have a good time.'

'You're the boss lady?'

Sophia laughed, the sound reaching all the way inside him and teasing at the edges of his mouth.

'Yes, I'm the boss lady.'

'One day I want to be the big boss lady...on the moon.'

Sophia laughed again, her hand reaching out to stroke Lily's cheek. 'Then remember what I said about your maths and your reading.'

'Maths *and* reading?'

Sophia nodded and Lily looked up at him. He was waiting for the eye roll; instead she hooked her tiny hand through his and looked back to Sophia with a firm nod. 'Okay.'

'Good girl.' She ruffled Lily's hair before rising up, her eyes finally coming back to his. They were still bright, but her cheeks had calmed, only a hint of pink remaining beneath the delicate sprinkling of freckles.

'I trust you have everything you need in your room,' she said smoothly, the difference in her marked. She was in work mode now and he found himself wanting the other version back, the version that had just spoken so kindly to his daughter.

'But if there is anything at all that you require, please don't hesitate to call down.' She gestured for them to leave the room. 'Shall we, Mr Mc-Gregor?'

'Jack, please.' Normally formal terms of address didn't bother him; he was used to it. In her case, though, it seemed he couldn't let it go.

He was treated to another flush of colour in her cheeks, something he was fast becoming attached to, and she cleared her throat. 'Jack.'

Better. Much better.

Her eyes evaded him now as she sought out her assistant manager. 'Andrew, could you see Jack and Lily to their room, please, and relieve Marie.'

'Of course.'

Jack looked to the elderly gentleman and knew who he'd rather be escorted by. Perhaps his lack of interest in the dating scene was taking its toll. It wasn't as if opportunities didn't present themselves but what had first been an avoidance of women, especially in the months following Elena's death, had now become a habit. Life was far less complicated when it was just him and Lily to think about. Him, Lily and work.

'It was a pleasure to meet you, Mr— *Jack*, and

Lily. I hope you enjoy your stay.' She turned and swept from the room, no backward glance. And he wanted one.

'Daddy?' Lily tugged on his hand and he looked down at her.

'Yes?'

'I think you should change her mind.'

He laughed, but inside he completely agreed with his little girl.

And what was that about?

He had no idea.

But the desire was there, all the same.

CHAPTER TWO

SOPHIA RUBBED THE back of her neck and stifled a yawn. Before her, the computer screen started to blur, facts and figures forming indistinct lines and making her squint. It was gone ten and she should have left work long ago but all that waited for her was an empty apartment and her thoughts. Neither of which she could bring herself to cope with.

Tomorrow would be better. Tomorrow it would be February, marking the end of another anniversary. Ten years since the death of her sister. A decade of guilt and grief. Time was supposed to heal. Make it easier. Soothe the horrors of the past. Whoever said that was either an idealist or a liar.

A short rap on the door put an end to her depressive stupor and she looked to it.

'Yes?'

The door opened and Andrew poked his head around. 'Isn't it time you left?'

'I will, soon.'

He nodded but didn't make to leave, his eyes narrowed on her instead. 'Mr McGregor seemed nice.'

Sophia's heart gave an involuntary flutter, just as it had every time she'd found herself reflecting on their little encounter that afternoon. 'Yes, and were they happy when you left?'

'Well, I think Ms Archer would've been happier to see the child disciplined more, but as far as their accommodation goes they're happy enough.'

'Good.'

'So, I'm off…' He hesitated on the threshold. 'You will go home soon?'

Sophia gave him a reassuring smile. 'Yes, *soon*.'

'Okay, goodnight.'

''Night.'

He pulled the door closed and Sophia looked back to her computer screen, starting to kill the applications still running. She was about to shut down her internet browser when the face of Jack McGregor came back to her, the instant effect he'd had on her pulse just as effective now.

She'd never felt anything like it. Ever. She was a twenty-four-year-old woman with zero relationship experience, zero experience of men really, unless you counted the odd fumbling kiss in her teens. She'd pretty much considered that part of her physical make-up dead, any frisson of excitement lost in her well-controlled exterior and the persistent ache left by the loss of Amy, her happy-go-lucky sister.

But she'd felt it looking into his eyes, she couldn't deny it. Not just the thrill, the kick to her pulse; there had been a connection she couldn't shake. It had taken her all to reinstate the professional front, turn down his offer of dinner and leave.

Was it the fact he had suffered too? The loss of someone he had loved? Was there some weird underlying connection drawing her to him?

She wasn't an old romantic. When her friends had dreamed of fairy-tale weddings, two-point-four children and happy-ever-afters she'd thrown herself into her studies, making sure she was the best she could possibly be, that she achieved and achieved. Not that it had made her home life easier.

No, she'd been invisible to her parents. It didn't matter what she did, what awards she won, what promotion she earned. She could never bring back her little sister, the one she should have been taking care of when it happened—an accident she herself had instigated.

That same wrenching motion took hold of her gut and her hand went to her stomach, her lungs dragging in air. It would pass. The nausea always did soon enough. But the force of it was always the same, the pain no less than it had been when she was fourteen.

But today…today she'd had a glimpse of an entirely different emotion, one that gave her hope that she had no right to feel, and her fingers moved to the keyboard, almost of their own volition, his name appearing letter by letter. She hit the enter key before she could reconsider and there he was, filling her screen: images across the top, article after article listed below.

What are you doing, Sophia?

It was likely he had no interest in her. Why would he? He was a billionaire businessman leading a life set so far apart from her own…but it didn't stop her looking, didn't stop her seeking the distraction he so readily represented, or preventing the spark he lit within her.

She smiled at the screen, her body indulging in the escapist fantasy he represented and for the first time in her life she understood the dreams of her peers in their teens.

Shame she was far too wise for dreams, far too weathered to find passion, fun and whatever else Jack had inspired in her. But sitting there in the privacy of her office she could pretend she was normal, that she was capable of more, that maybe, just maybe, she didn't have to be dead on the inside too.

Jack was at a loss.

He'd dealt with Connor and the unexpected hurdle in their takeover bid. He had calmed Ms

Archer to the point that she hadn't chosen to pack in the job altogether and he'd decided to give her one more chance. And he'd been on hand at bedtime, coaxing Lily into her pyjamas and bed without too much fuss. But his daughter's last words as he'd bade her goodnight echoed with his own internal plea.

Please can we see Sphea again?

He rarely had an interest in anyone outside of Lily, outside of work. The last time he had tried for more he'd been a disappointment, long before the hit-and-run, long before Lily even. He'd tried to make Elena happy, he truly had, but it had never been enough—*he* wasn't enough.

He raked his fingers through his hair and leaned forward in his chair, reaching out for the whisky decanter on his desk and pouring a decent measure.

The fact was he never wanted to be in that position again. He'd grown up with nothing. Put into care at the age of six when his mother had shown more interest in getting her next fix than feeding her own son. He'd spent his childhood acting out, angry at the world, at her, for being alone, unwanted and unloved. There had been the promise that his mother would get better, that she would have him back, until finally she'd died of an overdose when he was nine. No, he'd been destined for a troubled childhood of foster homes and he'd soon realised that if he ever wanted to gain control over his life he needed to take charge of his own destiny and that meant becoming financially independent.

He'd thrown himself into his studies, working hard to ensure he could stand alone, and on that journey he'd met Elena. A foster child like him, they'd been homed together at thirteen and grown close, their family history so similar it had given them a bond that no one could take away.

He'd sworn he'd take her with him, he'd look out for her; she too would escape the bad hand they'd been dealt. She'd loved him and he had loved her too, in so much as he could. Though over time it had become more like friendship—to him at any rate—only he hadn't realised it quickly enough.

The day she'd asked him to marry her he'd known it. He'd known it and couldn't bear the pain of telling her. And then she'd produced the pregnancy test, a shock to them both, and he'd known he could never tell her.

He'd set aside his own feelings to do right by her, as he'd always promised, and they'd married, they'd had Lily, and he had worked harder than ever. Longer hours, more trips away. Part avoidance. Part habit. But their relationship had suffered; she'd wanted more of him, more family time, more couple time, more love.

The night of the accident he'd been working late—another failed promise to come home in time for dinner. She'd left the food on the table, taken Lily in the buggy and headed out to the park. It was how he'd found the house when he'd returned home from the hospital, a sleeping Lily in his arms. Quiet. Dark. Cold.

He threw back the whisky, needing its burn to neutralise the churn in his gut.

Elena had been lonely. He'd *made* her lonely. She'd loved him and he'd repaid her with…what?

No, he didn't deserve another's love. Save for Lily's. He'd take that and give her back his all. She was his priority. The only one he needed to be concerned with.

So why did he want more time with Sophia? Why would he want to get mixed up in something that could only complicate things?

He clenched the whisky glass tighter in his hand and stared out unseeing at the impressive London skyline. The view that made the hotel penthouse one of the best in London was wasted on him right now. And just what would Ms Lambert say to that?

He conjured her up in his mind's eye—the appeal of her creamy, freckled skin, her over-bright blue eyes and that mass of red hair he could only imagine splayed out upon his pillow…and felt the heat of attraction he hadn't experienced in so long burning away the chill, the emptiness…and in Elena's city of all places. *Their* city.

His throat closed over, his hand pulsing around

the whisky glass as guilt swelled just as quickly, forcing hatred on its tail. Because he did hate London. It had been their home and she had died there. But it wasn't hate that had engulfed him the second he'd laid eyes on the fascinating hotel manager. No, it had been far more potent and far more disturbing than that.

It was also the reason he couldn't sleep. And drinking alone in his penthouse wasn't improving his mood. He should have gone to the gym rather than hit the bottle, but two whiskies in and exercise was out.

Perhaps the hotel bar would be preferable. The in-house pianist was talented and at least the gentle hum of people might distract him from the inner workings of his brain that seemed determined to flip-flop between the pain of the past and the potentially disruptive Ms Lambert.

Eleven o'clock. So much for leaving just after Andrew had bade her goodnight.

Instead, she'd lost herself in the enigma that was Mr McGregor—Jack.

Married to his childhood sweetheart, father to one girl and an orphan who'd come from nothing and made billions. It was the perfect fairy tale and the tabloids had capitalised on it, not holding back on the personal details they divulged either, worst of which was his mother's demise in a drug den, and that his father was unknown.

Her heart ached for him even as she read on. It seemed he fared better these days. No salacious gossip pertaining to his private life, no pictures of his daughter, no rumoured love interests since the passing of his wife. It was all business-or charity-related news and her admiration of him swelled.

Just what would it be like to sit across a table from this man and learn what made him tick, what made him the man he was today, to achieve all he had, to continue to achieve when he'd lost the closest person to him. His wife. The odd picture existed of them together at events. She had been beautiful, a statuesque blonde to his tall, dark good looks. But now she was gone, taken from their daughter before she'd had a chance to see her grow.

Sophia's eyes burned with unshed tears and she rubbed at them, refusing to submit. It didn't help to cry. She'd learned that over the years. It didn't change anything; it didn't bring anyone back.

She took a breath and let it shudder out of her. Tired. She was just tired. Time to go home and pour a nice glass of red and a stupidly hot bath. No more distracting herself with Tall, Dark and Handsome and his own personal tragedy. She had enough tragedy of her own to bear.

She pushed out of her chair and finally shut down her computer. Shouldering her handbag and hooking her coat over her arm, she headed out. At least it was late so maybe sleep would be forthcoming for a change and the nightmares non-existent.

She was halfway across the foyer when her eyes were drawn in the direction of the bar, to one lone figure in particular. Even from this distance she knew it was Jack.

He was leaning back in one of the plush arm-chairs, drink in hand, one leg crossed over the other, his ankle resting upon his knee. He'd lost the suit jacket and tie, his shirt now unbuttoned at the collar and framing his broad shoulders, his posture the only relaxed thing about him because his eyes told another story. Trained on the pianist playing in the corner of the soft-lit room, they were intense, inward, thoughtful, a frown creas-ing his brow as he stroked his forefinger across his lips.

She should move but her feet felt glued to the floor. And then he stilled, the finger pausing over his lips as his eyes shifted and connected directly with her own. Her belly came alive, tiny little flut-ters erupting all the way to her throat.

She tried for a smile, swallowing back the nerves and whatever else her body was in the mood to feel. She gave a nod which was meant as a silent goodnight, but instead of leaving she headed for him. What possessed her she didn't know, but the second his lips curved upwards her body gained a will of its own.

He stood as she neared. 'Sophia, it's good to see you again.'

His words lit her up from top to toe, whether he meant them or not. And how could he when she was no one special?

'And you.' She gestured to the drink he'd placed on the small round table beside him. 'Enjoying a nightcap?'

'The bar's finest. Can I tempt you to join me?'

Her eyes darted to his, an impulsive 'no' dying on her lips as she heard herself say, 'I wouldn't want to intrude.'

'You're not.'

She looked back to the foyer, to the exit just beyond and where she should be heading.

'Unless you count the fact you're taking my mind off my thoughts, which isn't a bad thing, believe me.'

His honesty called her eyes back to his and then she saw it, in the lines around his eyes, in their stormy glint—the same kind of pain, the same need for distraction that she felt.

'It's late and I really should go.'

'A quick one then…just to say thank you for today?'

She couldn't say yes. He was a client. This was her hotel. It wasn't the done thing. Only the same reasoning she'd used earlier was weaker now, in the lateness of the day, the intimacy of the bar and its lighting, with him filling her vision and drowning out the past. Perhaps for both of them.

'Okay.' She nodded, her lips wavering into a smile. 'A small Shiraz…please.'

His grin reignited the nervous flutter in her belly. And it was nerves. Just nerves.

'Great, take a seat.'

She did as he asked, sitting in the vacant chair positioned at an angle alongside his own and tried to relax.

Relax? You should be leaving. No good can come of you indulging yourself in the fantasy world he represents. It's not real. Not for you.

'It's on its way.'

His voice was real enough; she mentally fought back as he returned, closing her mind to everything but his presence.

'I hope I'm not keeping you from anything?'

She laughed at the very idea and watched him settle back in his seat. It was disconcerting, bizarre even. It was her hotel and yet he looked more at home here than she did, perched on the edge of her seat as if at any moment she might bolt.

She shifted back, resting her coat over the arm of her chair and crossing her legs. She wanted to appear just as at home, just as calm, just as in control, when she knew she wasn't.

'If by that you're asking whether I have a partner waiting up for me…' She lowered her bag to the floor, her eyes coming back to his as she straightened up. 'No, you don't need to worry about that.'

'Good.'

Good?

She narrowed her eyes. 'Are you flirting with me, Mr McGregor?'

Heavens, where had that come from?

Not only the question but the realisation that she wanted him to flirt with her. She was in trouble and sinking deeper, when she should be at home, running that bath and forgetting her problems in the sanctuary of solitude.

His long, deep laugh put the brakes on her escape plan, the sound provoking her already racing pulse. 'It's Jack, remember, and I suppose I was...'

Sophia tilted her head to the side, her curiosity aroused by his tone, his hesitancy. She couldn't imagine Jack being less than one hundred per cent sure of himself. Maybe she wasn't the only one struggling with this surprising connection. It actually made her feel better. Not a lot, but enough to ask, 'Why do I get the impression you've surprised yourself with that admission?'

He held her eye, silent for a beat. 'In all honesty, I'm a little rusty.'

Her smile was slow, growing with her confidence. 'You and me both.'

And there she went again, encouraging him when she knew she shouldn't, but she couldn't stop.

'I can't believe a woman like you could be all that rusty.'

'A woman like me never really got started.'

The air seemed to crackle in the silence that descended, a stream of unspoken thoughts passing between them.

'Jack, I—' She broke off as her drink arrived. She glanced up at her head barman with a smile. 'Thank you, Peter.'

'You're welcome.' He walked discreetly away, for which she was grateful.

She picked up the glass, took a much-needed sip and regathered her wits to tell him what needed to be said. That she didn't do flirting, or any kind of dating for that matter. Certainly not with the clientele, or anyone come to that. But as her eyes returned to his, now almost black in the low light, she found her voice failed her.

'Jack, you…what?' He gestured at her with one hand, drawing her eye to those long, lithe fingers that looked so capable, so strong, and the heat spread from her core to her cheeks and she swallowed, hard.

'I'm not sure this is wise.'

'No,' he said softly. 'You're probably right.'

Disappointment sneaked its way in, and she found her second sip of wine far harder to take than her first.

'And yet you still came over?'

Her cheeks flushed deeper. 'It would have been rude not to.'

'Is that the only reason? You didn't want to appear rude?'

She felt her eyes widen, her heart pulse in her chest. No, it wasn't, was it?

The fantasy she'd been harbouring in her office collided with reality, her lie catching in her tone as she said, 'I wanted to see how Lily and Ms Archer were faring after their little adventure.'

'They're fine, thank you for asking.' His lips quirked, the spark in his eyes telling her he'd seen her lie for what it was. 'However, me, not so much.'

Her brow pulled together. 'Really, in what way?'

'It seems my daughter's high opinion of me has taken something of a knock.'

She could sense where this was heading, knew she should put a stop to it, but the thrill of it, of what he might admit, had her pushing for more. 'And why's that?'

'She's taken quite a shine to you and she's not impressed that I failed to secure her a thank-you dinner.'

She chuckled softly. 'Why does it sound like both you and your daughter are used to getting what you want?'

'Because we are.' He shrugged, his easy grin setting her belly on fire. 'What can I say? People are powerless in the face of our McGregor charm.'

'The McGregor charm?' She laughed again. It seemed Jack had the ability to lift her mood so completely with his boasted charm, no matter how strung-out she was.

'What?' He raised his brow at her, his eyes dancing. 'Are you questioning its existence?'

'Moi?' She pressed her palm to her chest in mock sincerity. 'I wouldn't dare.'

Now he laughed, the sound resonating through her and making her feel so very alive.

'You could help me get out of trouble very easily, you know.'

She stilled, her smile as genuine as she felt. 'Is that you asking me to dinner again?'

'Is that you saying you will agree this time?' he quipped, his hopeful expression weakening the last of her resolve.

'Dinner with you *and* Lily?'

'Yes, she can be our chaperone.'

'Are we in need of a chaperone?'

Too quick. Too feisty. Too full-on, Sophia!

Something flashed in his gaze, something akin to the heat streaking right to her toes as she realised she couldn't take back her reckless words and knew she didn't want to either.

'So, what do you say?'

She didn't know whether she should be disappointed or relieved that he didn't answer her question. Not directly at any rate.

But what should she say?

No, because the chemistry between us is scaring the life out of me.

No, because I'm messed-up and in no place for whatever this is.

No, because...just because.

'You know, I really am starting to question my charm.'

His grin, filled with the very charm she'd brought into question, seared away any intention of saying no.

And what was there to say no to when she thought about it rationally?

She enjoyed his company. She'd enjoyed Lily's company that afternoon. Would it really be so bad to go to dinner? What was the worst that could happen with his daughter present?

She smiled and raised her glass to her lips, enjoying the anticipation heating the air between them. This was fun. So much fun. And fun wasn't something she'd had in a long time.

'Come on, one dinner and you'll make both mine and Lily's day.'

She knew she'd regret it later, but...

'Okay, Jack, dinner it is.'

CHAPTER THREE

As far as Fridays went, today was certainly up there with the worst and she was late. Really late. She'd agreed to meet Jack in the foyer at six-thirty but it was now gone seven and she was having to call his room to delay it another thirty minutes at least.

'Jack, I'm so sorry,' she rushed out as soon as he answered. 'I'm still tied up.'

'It's okay.'

In the background she could hear an excited Lily asking if it was Sphea and she closed her eyes briefly, shutting down the guilt.

'I can deal with this,' Andrew said before her.

'No, it's fine,' she mouthed, adding into the receiver, 'Maybe we could do this another night?'

She cringed after she said it, her ears straining for his response. She knew she was running scared, but she'd had time to sleep on it, a day to think without him in front of her…

'No, we'll do it tonight, just let me know when you're ready.'

Her shoulders relaxed and tensed up again just as quickly. 'But it's already past seven. Surely Lily needs to eat and get to bed.'

'Let me worry about her and you get yourself sorted.'

She said, 'Okay,' as she hung up although she was far from okay. The truth was her common sense had returned the second she'd been outside of Jack McGregor's field of charm, and she'd known she couldn't indulge this strange fantasy that had overcome her.

She was Sophia Lambert, destined to live and die alone for what she'd done. It was the very same reason she couldn't go back home and visit her parents. To see Mum and Dad, the way they would embrace her and pretend to forgive. She couldn't. Just. Couldn't.

And the more she kept her distance from people, the less likely she was to suffer a similar loss again. It was how she lived her life, how she had to live it.

'Seriously, Sophia, if I'd known you had plans I never would have brought this to you in the first place,' Andrew stressed, wearing his own look of guilt. 'We're more than capable of dealing with it.'

He was right. They were. And yet here she was, insisting it be her. Seeking a delay that gave her the distance she needed.

'I know you are.' She strode forward and gave him a reassuring smile. 'But you should have clocked off an hour ago. You know Cassie will be waiting for you.'

Cassie, his wife, always planned a candlelit dinner on Friday nights and Sophia knew how much both she and Andrew valued that tradition.

'*Go,*' she insisted, spying the continued hesitation in his gaze.

He shook his head in surrender. 'Okay, I'm going, but get this delegated and get yourself off. You need fun too.'

His grin was warm, but she could see the concern that cast a shadow over it. She didn't need Andrew to worry about her. She was fine. At least she would be after the night was done and she could go back to life as normal. Why had she even agreed in the first place?

Silly question. She couldn't think past the chaos that kicked up inside when she was around Jack.

She watched Andrew go, wondering what it would be like to have that kind of companionship and unconditional love to go home to. Was she a fool to reject it at every turn?

Her phone rang again and she pushed the thought aside. Just work—focus on that.

And she did.

It was almost eight by the time she caught a breather to think about Jack and his daughter. Her inner self laughed at her. *Who are you kidding? You've been forcing yourself not to think about them all evening.*

And Lily didn't deserve such behaviour. Neither did Jack. It wasn't his fault she was in a tizz over the way he made her feel.

She picked up the phone and dialled his room, anxiously rubbing at her neck as she waited.

'Hello?'

The fine hairs beneath her fingers pricked up, her heart tripping over itself and all from his simple hello.

'Hi.' She swallowed. 'It's Sophia.'

'Hey.'

She could hear the smile in his voice, imagined him standing before her and basking in its glow. And there she was, drowning in a sea of sensation and losing her mind all over again.

'I'm ready if you are.' She sounded breathless, her lungs struggling to function past the churn of nerves...or was it excitement?

'Great, I'll see you in the foyer in five.'

'Great,' she parroted, lowering the phone and staring at it as if she couldn't believe this was happening. Any of it.

The evening truly was set. She was going to dinner with a guy who was the stuff of heroes in one of her favourite romance novels and his charming daughter—*Single Dad meets Lonely Hotelier*—she could see it now in all its fanciful glory and pinched herself back to reality.

For the first time in her adult life Sophia was going to take a risk and let go for a night. She was going to have some fun, safe in the company of Lily, and then tomorrow she would move on. Simple.

Only when she got to the foyer there was no sign of them. The lift pinged its arrival and the doors opened.

There he was, dominating the opening, her eyes so caught up in him that she didn't notice the lack of mini-McGregor. Not until he was striding for her, the designer cut to his deep blue suit complementing his smooth, confident stride, his white shirt open at the collar, his grey eyes sharp against his dark skin and pinned wholly on her.

She frowned, looked to his left, his right, behind. She wet her lips. 'No Lily?'

He paused before her, his smile bordering on sheepish. 'I took your advice and fed her early. She's now tucked up in bed as she should be and I'm all yours… I mean…well, you know what I mean.'

Her cheeks coloured, the warmth spreading through her belly and smothering her nerves. 'You should have eaten with her, not waited for me. We could have postponed.'

'No chance.' He grimaced, his hand running through his hair that refused to be tamed and her palms tingled, itching to try. 'The only way I could get Lily fed and into bed was by assuring her we would still go out to dinner.'

She gave a shaky laugh. 'She has you wrapped around her little finger.'

'Don't all daughters?'

She thought of her own father and banished him from her mind just as swiftly. 'I hope she wasn't too disappointed?'

'No, she just sees it as a reason for us to get together again.'

Her heart skipped a beat. Pleasure, quickly followed by panic. 'Again?'

He chuckled. 'Do you have to look so unsettled by the idea?'

'Sorry, I'm just thinking… I'm sure you have more important things to be doing while in London.'

'Let us McGregors be the judge of that, hey?'

His light-hearted tone and the appreciative heat of his gaze worked together to lure her into feeling almost worthy of this evening, of a date with someone as impressive as him.

'Shall we?'

It took her a second to register his gesture to leave, another for his arm to curve around her and for his palm to settle against her lower back. The warmth of his touch soothed away her anxiety and slowly she turned on her heel and walked with him to the door, her head awash with questions.

Would it hurt, just for one night, to pretend it was all possible? To pretend it was a date? A real date? To go with the flow, go with…? His fingers fluttered against her lower back, reminding her of their presence, their effect, and her breath caught with her silent agreement.

When going with the flow felt this good, how could she possibly fight it?

'I hope you like Chinese.'

'Hmm?' was all she could manage as she focused on keeping her legs moving and not turning to jelly beneath her.

'This restaurant used to be a favourite of mine,' he added.

'Uh-huh.' *Oh, goodness, Sophia, is that really the best you can do?* 'I'm so hungry I could eat pretty much anything right now.'

She flicked him a look, saw his eyebrow raise at her impulsive statement and snapped her eyes back ahead. He thought she meant him. *Him.*

She nearly swallowed her tongue and threw her attention to the night doorman instead. 'Evening, Henry.'

'Miss Lambert.' He held the door open for them both and smiled. 'Have a good evening.'

'Thank you,' Jack said, his focus returning to Sophia. 'I'd tell you to put your coat on but my driver's waiting for us and the car will be warm.'

He looked to a sleek black car parked up in the circular courtyard, its driver, dressed in livery, already pulling open the rear door.

Wow. The number of times she had greeted or bade farewell to influential clients in this entrance, dreamed of how their lives would be, so different to her own, and now here she was, doing the exact same thing.

Her grip on reality really was wavering, but in that moment, as she thanked his driver and slipped inside the luxurious interior of his car, she didn't care.

Reality could wait a few more hours at least…

Jack waited for her to get settled into the back seat before joining her a respectful distance away, but her presence radiated down his side, his pulse hammering in a way it hadn't since…since for ever.

He watched her out of the corner of his eye as she played with her fingers upon her lap, her attention on the outside world as his driver pulled out into the traffic.

She wore a similar dress to the previous day, only now she'd lost the ID badge. Her hair was once again knotted up high, her make-up sparse and natural, and her ears were adorned with small pearl droplets that drew his attention to her long, slender neck. She had an effortless poise about her that made her as elegant as any date he'd had before.

Though this wasn't a date. Nothing of the sort.

It was a thank-you meal to keep his daughter happy.

He just had to keep reminding himself of that fact.

'Something tells me you work late a lot?' It was a question aimed to distract himself from his thoughts, but as she looked to him, her eyes sparkling with humour, he could no longer deny the reason he was here was because, above all else, he wanted to be.

And he wanted it to be a date, to take her out to dinner regardless of whether it was wise or sensible, without guilt.

'Something tells me you do too.' Her voice was light, teasing, and he found himself grinning.

'Fair point.'

She returned his smile, her fingers ceasing their nervous play. 'I take it you're in London on business?'

'Yes, that's right. I was hoping it would be a week, but it's looking more like two now.'

She frowned a little. 'You're in a hurry to leave then?'

'Is it that obvious?'

'You were the one who said you *hoped* to be gone sooner,' she reminded him, not missing a beat. 'I assume that's because you're *wanting* to be gone.'

She waved a hand through the air and he had to stop himself from frowning as he thought about the reason he wanted to be gone. He didn't want to think about it. He didn't want anything to put a damper on their evening, not now they were heading out together. Alone. Just the two of them.

And there came the guilt again...the timely reminder of Elena and his biggest failure. He glanced out of the window and London looked back at him, full of its memories. He breathed through it and schooled his expression.

'I was,' he said, facing her again. 'London isn't... London isn't exactly a city I'm fond of.'

Her eyes scanned his face, her curiosity at his remark obvious, but he did the same, taking advantage of her attention to drink her in, her natural beauty, her appeal that warmed him all the way to the bone, and he realised that London looked slightly less grey now. 'But perhaps staying longer isn't such a bad thing.'

Her eyes met his and he added carefully, 'Lily certainly likes the idea.'

She nodded, her smile full of affection. 'She seems like a great kid.'

'That she is.'

'Do you travel a lot with her?'

'Quite a bit.'

'So where's home when you're not travelling?'

Home? Nowhere. Not since London, not since Elena. A cold sweat instantly spread, the hairs at his nape prickling against the crisp collar of his shirt and sending his eyes back to the outside world, safe from her astute gaze.

He clenched his hand into the soft leather seat and tried to keep his voice neutral. 'We don't have one as such. I have headquarters in various continents and I move between them depending on where I'm needed most.'

She was quiet for a while and he took the time to regain that sense of ease, to put the past to bed for a few hours at least.

'She must be well travelled for a… How old is she?'

'Five—she's six in a few weeks.' And she was excited about it too, birthdays becoming a bigger deal now. His heart and body softened as he remembered their conversation just last night and how they had to count the number of sleeps remaining.

'Ah, a birthday—how lovely! And what has she asked for?'

'A pony.'

Sophia's laugh tinkled through the car, taking away the last of his unease with it. '*Every* little girl goes through that phase.'

'You too?'

'Oh, yes, my sister and I…' A slight tremor entered her voice and she shook her head, her throat bobbing as her eyes flitted away for a second, and when they came back there was a sheen that hadn't existed before. But still she smiled, the gesture such a contrast to her sudden sadness. 'We begged for one, just one to share if we couldn't have one each.'

He couldn't take his eyes from the look in hers. 'And did you get your wish?' he asked softly.

She shook her head and he knew the sheen of tears had nothing to do with the pony. He wanted to ask her what was wrong, but he didn't want to make it worse. He didn't want to upset her. He tried to think of something else to say—anything to fill the void, to distract her—but the look in her eyes haunted him. It made him want to delve deeper, have her talk, and in turn he could offer... offer what? Comfort? Distraction from whatever this was?

His eyes fell to her lips and he felt the pull swell exponentially, felt it wrap around them, drawing them closer. Did she feel it too?

'So...' her voice drew him up sharply, his eyes lifting to hers to catch the way her lashes fluttered, her breath shaky as she visibly sought to regain control '...is she getting a pony?'

He gave a laugh that sounded more like a bark as he tried to relax into his seat. What was wrong with him? He was used to beautiful women up close and personal, but never had he felt so out of control of his senses.

Maybe it was the hint of trauma, of darkness he glimpsed in her too. The one thing he could understand, feel connected to.

'Hardly.' He raked a hand over his hair and looked to the window, to the far less evocative passing world. 'They don't exactly fit in a suitcase, and she has no need for one, not when I bought her an entire stud farm last year.'

'You bought her what?' she choked out, half-laughing, half-incredulous, calling his gaze back to her.

'Last year she asked for a horse,' he explained with a shrug, 'and it seemed like a wise investment opportunity.'

'I don't think she was thinking about its investment potential.'

He grinned now. 'No, that much is true, but she has one of the racehorses named in her honour and she gets to sit on him occasionally.'

'Right…okay…' She gave a downward smile, her head nodding as her eyes twinkled under the passing streetlights. No sadness now.

'What?'

'Nothing.'

'What?'

'Don't you think she was looking more for a pet, a friend of some sort?'

'Perhaps.'

'Maybe she thinks asking for a pony will give her that. I'm surprised she hasn't asked for a puppy.'

'Oh, she's asked for one of those too.'

'And it's a no?'

'Again, not suitcase-friendly and it wouldn't be fair to lug it from country to country, not to mention the vaccinations, the pet passport, the poo...' He shuddered. 'No, it's a definite no.'

A crease formed between her brows and she looked desperate to say something.

'What is it?' he probed when she wasn't forthcoming.

'It's nothing.' She caught her bottom lip in her teeth and looked to the window.

'Nothing again, hey?' He had to drag his eyes from her mouth, from the plump flesh caught in her teeth, taunting him with the urge to run his thumb over it, release it...kiss it. He cleared his suddenly tight throat. 'Well, if that's your "nothing" face, I'd love to see what you look like when you *are* thinking something.'

She gave him a guilty smile, snuffing out the desire with rising curiosity. Just what was she thinking?

'It doesn't feel my place to say.'

He tensed. 'Now I really am curious.'

'Well...it can't be easy on her, travelling all the time.'

'She's seeing the world. There aren't many five-year-olds that can claim to have visited as many incredible cities as she has.'

'But what does she do for schooling?'

The tension ratcheted up. 'She's taught by Ms Archer.'

Her brow lifted. 'She's home-schooled?'

'You say that like it's a bad thing, but what other option is there when we travel so much?'

'It's…well, it's just…when does she get to see other children, have play dates, that sort of thing?'

He frowned at her, the tension making him snap. 'My daughter wants for nothing. She's kept safe, she's well educated, and I'd like to think well-rounded too.'

She shook her head softly. 'But it must be lonely for her? Especially if you don't have a base, a place to call home.'

Surely home was where he was. It was why he took her everywhere with him. He wouldn't be the poor excuse for a father that he'd once been, always absent, always late.

'It's a well-known fact that children are quite resilient to change.' He knew he sounded petulant, defensive, but she'd got his hackles up.

She studied him silently and he wondered whether she would argue more, dreading what she would say next, but instead she nodded.

'I'm sure you're right. What do I know after all?' She shrugged. 'I'm not a parent and she is lovely, really truly…'

She looked back to the window, but her words hung over him. No one had ever questioned his parenting before, not since Elena and her desperate plea for him to be around more. And now he was never far away from Lily—they had weekends and bedtimes.

He could sense Sophia's thoughts still whirring away and the need to defend himself, to explain, had him opening his mouth to speak but she got there first. 'So what have you got against London?'

It was the last thing he'd expected and he was ill-prepared for it, the direct hit winding him as his chest squeezed tight, the fateful night replaying in his head in freefall. The blood left his face and he saw her own eyes widen, her hand reaching out to softly touch his arm, sending an aftershock rippling through him, a confusing mix of heat teasing at the chill.

'I'm so sorry,' she whispered. 'I shouldn't have asked.'

He was slow to respond. Slow to quash the swirl of emotion inside, slow to adjust to the warmth spreading beneath her touch. He never spoke of it. London. The past. Elena.

'I read about your…your wife.' Her eyes wavered over his face, projecting and evoking so much emotion that he couldn't break free of it to speak. Thinking about Elena was one thing. Talking to Sophia of her was another.

'I don't talk about it.' His voice was tight, dead, and he watched her nod, the sheen returning to her gaze.

'I understand.'

And then he saw it reappear in her gaze, heard it in her words. She didn't simply understand; she felt it. She felt it as only someone who'd been there could. She'd lost someone too. He knew it just as clearly as if she'd told him so herself. And he forgot his own pain in hers.

'Who was it?'

Her lips parted in surprise, a subtle frown marring her brow. 'Who?'

'You've lost someone too.' He covered her hand upon his arm as she shook her head, her pain tugging at a part of him he'd long since thought dead. 'I can tell, Sophia. You don't have to talk about it, not if you don't want to, but...'

She took a shaky breath, her fingers trembling beneath his as she swallowed and lifted her chin a little. 'My sister.'

'When?'

She blinked back tears as she looked to him and the air caught in his lungs, her beauty all the more powerful for her sorrow. 'Ten years ago.'

'And yet it feels like yesterday?'

She nodded, the knowledge passing between them, the shared understanding, the bond growing.

'It doesn't matter how much time passes,' he said, the words easing out with their connection, 'how many times I return to London, to where we lived together...' He shook his head. *We?* More like *she*... He'd never been around. Absentee husband. Absentee father. His throat closed over. He couldn't face up to his failings, not in front of Sophia, not when her soft blue gaze offered up sympathy he had no right to accept.

He closed his fingers around her hand and squeezed gently, throwing the focus onto her. 'I'm sorry you lost your sister.'

She gave a small smile. 'Isn't it funny how we all say we're sorry, like we're in some way to blame for their death?'

His blood ran cold. He *was* to blame for Elena's. If he'd just come home in time for dinner, if he hadn't taken that last phone call, if he hadn't ignored her ringing him...

'I guess it's just a catch-all term, a way to express our sadness at the news of someone's passing, the pain of those left behind, but you hear it so much you become numb to it.'

'Yes.' He felt her fingers flex beneath his seconds before she pulled away, saw her eyes cloud over as she twisted her hands together again.

'What happened?'

She stilled and he cursed his lack of tact. He never should have asked. But he wanted to know. He wanted to reach out for her once more, to pull her hand back, to offer and take comfort. Even though, to all intents and purposes, they were nothing more than strangers.

Only she didn't feel like a stranger and he had no idea what to make of that. He felt exposed, vulnerable, as if he'd opened up a part of himself that he always kept well hidden. And he could sense she had too.

Maybe that was why he couldn't let it go. Why, when his brain told him to change the subject, to pull away from the personal, something more powerful had him wanting her to open up. To talk to him.

He was a hypocrite. He didn't want to talk about Elena and yet he was pushing her to talk about her sister. 'I'm sorry. You really don't have to talk about—'

'It was a sledging accident, ten years ago yesterday in fact...' Even though her eyes were on her hands, he could visualise the pain in them as she spoke, her words whisper-soft. 'It was my fault too. I'd taken her out on my own while Mum and Dad were busy with friends. We were only supposed to be gone an hour, but we were having too much fun, and she begged me for a go on her own, just one... It seemed harmless enough. I'd done it a thousand times before, so I sat her in and gave her a push—' She broke off, her body shuddering, her head lifting to look out of the window. 'She came off and hit her head on a rock hidden in the snow.'

His gut turned over with sickening force as the scene played out in his mind. 'How old was she?'

'Seven.' It shuddered out of her.

Seven. Barely older than his Lily. His gut rolled

anew, her pain feeding his own, and he couldn't hold back any longer. He reached out for her hand. 'It doesn't make it your fault. It was an accident, a tragic accident, surely you can see that?'

'But if I hadn't taken her out, if we'd only stayed indoors, if I hadn't said yes to that last ride, if I hadn't pushed her...' Her voice trailed off and he grasped both of her hands in his.

'Hindsight is a powerful thing, Sophia. We can learn from it, but you shouldn't let it torment you. It can't change the past.'

He should try telling himself the same too. Only he deserved to suffer. She didn't. Maybe it was the guilt that bound them and not the loss. No matter how undeserving hers was.

Her eyes snapped to his, adjusted, and then she was breathing deeply and blowing it out. 'And you really didn't need to know any of that. Sorry, let's just—'

He squeezed her hands, silencing her apology. 'I wanted to know.'

The silence settled around them, neither needing to speak, and the desire to draw her into him was there, aching in his arms, his chest.

She shook her head a little. 'I really don't do this normally.'

'Do what?' Though he could see what she meant in the surprise widening her eyes.

'Talk about the past, the accident...'

'It's not good to keep it all locked inside.'

Says the man who never talks of Elena.

'It seems we have quite the pasts to share,' she said quietly.

'Yes… I suppose we do.'

But her past…hers was the true pain of loss, shrouded in a guilt she shouldn't feel. Not like his guilt. His was deserved and it was the reason he couldn't accept her sympathy. Or anyone's love, for that matter.

With Elena he'd not only proved himself incapable of loving another, he'd proved himself unworthy of it too. He hadn't deserved her, and he certainly didn't deserve Sophia now.

He withdrew his hands and sat back in his seat once more.

He didn't deserve anyone.

CHAPTER FOUR

Sophia was in heaven.

It was the only way to describe the candlelit luxury of her surroundings and the calibre of the man sitting opposite her. No amount of reminding herself that this was temporary, just a thank-you meal to keep his daughter sweet, could dissuade her from getting wrapped up in him and his world.

As for the restaurant, everyone in the service industry knew of it with its numerous awards, accolades and several-months-long waiting list. She shouldn't really be surprised that Jack of all people had managed to secure a last-minute reservation, although people like him probably had a table kept in their name just on the off-chance they'd swing by. They'd certainly made him— *no, the two of them*—feel like royalty the second they'd arrived.

She spooned up her decadent chocolate dessert and in spite of being stuffed to the brim she couldn't resist its rich, salty-sweet goodness. Much as she couldn't resist discreetly devouring the sight of the man who'd recommended it. And with the wine, the pleasurable food and his stimulating conversation she was getting less discreet by the mouthful.

Now, as her eyes lifted to his, she paused, the spoon hovering halfway to her mouth. He was watching her, the dark intensity in his gaze making her pulse dance.

'What?' she asked, lowering the spoon just a little.

'You like your food.'

It was an observation, a simple statement of fact, but her cheeks burned. Her mother's teasing coming back from their childhood: *Did you inhale it?*

'I'm sorry.'

She placed the spoon back on the plate and smoothed her palm over her belly, her eyes falling away from his. Thoughts of her family always made her stomach swim. Seconds ago, she'd been floating in the clouds, loving every second, now she plummeted back to earth with a bump.

His grin was as swift as the shake of his head. 'Don't apologise.'

He leaned forward, his elbows pressing into the table as he rested his chin on his folded hands, that intense gaze still on her and making her forget the momentary nausea. 'It's a nice change, eating with someone who doesn't play with their food.'

'Are we back to talking about Lily again?'

He gave a soft laugh. 'No, she's as eager as you… I meant—' He broke off, another shake of his head.

'You meant…?'

Leaning back in his seat, he took up the napkin and raised it to his lips. Her eyes traced the move, the swipe of the cotton against their teasing curve, their appealing softness… What would it feel like to press her own lips against them, to catch the lower one in hers, to lick…? Promptly, she lifted her spoon and stuffed it inside her own mouth. There would be no kissing, no licking, no nothing.

She feasted on the dessert, slowly savouring the taste explosion as she tried to douse the heat unfurling low in her belly. But it was no use. It continued to flare, stoked by the way his own eyes watched her devouring the heady chocolate.

'I was going to say…' his voice had turned gruff, its edge at odds with the calm way in which he folded the napkin onto his plate '… it makes a change from the women I'm used to eating with.'

She felt the oddest spark of jealousy and quickly stamped it out with another spoon of heaven. Her taste buds sang while her brain talked her down. He wasn't hers to get jealous over. He never would be. It was ridiculous even to feel it.

But she had.

So much for not getting carried away. First kissing fantasies, and now jealousy! She wanted to roll her eyes at herself.

'Do you date often then?' The question came out smoothly, controlled, just as she'd hoped, but his sudden frown had her worrying she'd over-stepped.

'No.'

It was abrupt, severe. Was he thinking of his wife again?

In the car she'd felt his grief, seen it echoed back at her when she'd told him things she'd never told another soul because she'd been powerless to stop the words from flowing. She'd felt the con-nection, the understanding, the ability to let go of it just a little with someone who had also loved and lost.

'Not a lot anyway. I don't really have the time,' he added, softer now. 'Work takes up most of it, Lily the rest.'

Her heart eased a little, her smile lifting with it. 'I can believe it.'

'What about you?' He held her eye, the can-dlelight flickering in the darkened depths of his, making her forget how to breathe, how to blink, his attention making her feel almost drunk with it.

'Me?' She was stalling but, despite how much she'd already opened up to him, she wasn't ready to confess the sorry state of her love life. Not that she'd ever considered it 'sorry' before…

'Yes,' he pressed. 'You're beautiful, intelligent,

quite the catch. I'm sure you must get invited out often.'

Beautiful. Intelligent. Quite the catch.

Now she laughed, her head shaking incredulously as she covered her mouth with her hand. 'You, Mr McGregor, really are a charmer.'

'I only speak the truth.'

Did he? Was that really how he saw her?

She didn't like the way her body reacted to the idea. No, correction. She *loved* how her body reacted, and that was the problem.

'Sorry. I've made you uncomfortable.'

Was she really that obvious? Or did he just have a knack for reading her?

'You haven't. Or, rather, you have, but it's not your fault,' she assured him, taking up her wine glass for a confidence-boosting gulp. She had no need to lie. It wasn't as if she was there to impress him. And soon he would be gone, and she would be forgotten, so she might as well be honest. 'Truth is, I've never dated.'

His eyes widened, his shock permeating the air and making her cheeks burn anew in spite of her confident mental reasoning seconds before.

'*Never?*'

She shook her head.

'I take it you've always been in relationships instead. Friends that became more?'

His voice drifted off at the continued shaking of her head.

'No...*relationships*?'

She swallowed another sip of wine, knowing full well that her skin likely matched the blazing colour of her hair now. And she could hardly backtrack; she'd already said too much.

'I've always worked hard,' she tried to explain, grateful that her voice was level enough, her eyes still fixed on his, 'whether it was studying for exams at school, university or pushing my career, and I haven't had the time for it.'

'But...there must have been someone...at some point?'

She shook her head. 'You can consider yourself my first date—date-that's-not-a-date,' she swiftly added.

He studied her for so long, his face unreadable and, boy, was she trying. He was probably assessing her V plates right now and labelling her as some kind of freak.

'It's not that weird, surely?' She took another swig of wine. 'It's not like I've sprouted three heads.'

She was trying to lighten the mood and was relieved when he laughed. She wanted their easy footing back. They'd enjoyed it all through dinner when they'd talked of work, Lily, favourite foods, nothing serious. Not like in the car...

She shifted in her seat as she felt a line being drawn in the virtual sand. One side safe, platonic, friendly. The other... She wet her lips.

She knew which side her body wanted to be on.

And it wasn't the same as her single, solitary head.

'No, definitely not three heads…' His eyes fell to her recently glossed mouth. 'But you are quite fascinating, Ms Lambert.'

Jack watched her lips part, her cheeks flush deeper, their freckled warmth a delightful contrast to her sparkling blue gaze. Did she really have no idea how beautiful she was? That the reason her confession stunned him came from his disbelief that a woman with her qualities had avoided anything close to a relationship all these years? And what a waste that was…

'Fascinating?' She averted her eyes for a second, reached for her wine glass and took another sip, the rich red liquid disappearing swiftly now that their conversation had taken a more personal turn.

'You, Jack…' she waved the glass at him '… really are a master of flirtation… Rusty, nuh-uh.'

She shook her head as she made reference to their conversation the previous night, but he didn't comment, only asked the question he was eager to have answered now. 'How old are you?'

'Okay, scratch that last one,' she scoffed. 'Didn't your mother ever teach you not to ask a woman her age?'

She paled as soon as the words were out, her

wine glass deposited and her hand reaching across the table to rest upon his arm. 'I'm so sorry. I shouldn't have… I forgot, I didn't think—'

'Hey, it's fine,' he assured her, cutting off her panicked apology that she needn't give. 'I've been fielding questions like that for years; it's second nature now. Am I to take it you've been reading up on me?' He cocked an eyebrow at her, projecting a jovial arrogance in the hope that she would see that her words didn't sting.

The colour returned to her cheeks just as quickly, her hand pulling away to stroke the back of her neck. 'Maybe…just a little.'

'A little?'

'Okay, a lot… I happen to find you quite fascinating too, Jack.'

His eyes were lost in the blazing sincerity of hers, his ears ringing with the heat of her admission. *Touché*.

'You fancy taking a stroll before I take you home?'

He wasn't ready to be out of her company and was relieved to see her smile.

'I'd like that and… I'm twenty-four.'

'Twenty-four?' He raised his brow. 'That's quite an achievement, to get where you have at your age.'

'Now you sound patronising.'

He laughed at the scowl she sent him and gestured over her head for the bill, his eyes coming back to her, appreciative, sincere. 'No, I'm just impressed. I have almost ten years on you to get where I have.'

'Yes, well, I can't see me getting anywhere close to you in another twenty, let alone ten. Try as I might.' She winked on the last, her easy laughter carrying across the table and warming him through.

'Your parents must be proud?'

The second his words registered, he felt the sudden chill that came over her, her words wooden as she said, 'I guess.'

'You guess?' Had she lost them as well as her sister? Had he inadvertently put his foot in it too? 'I'm sorry, are they…are they not around any more?'

She took a breath and looked away, a hand smoothing over her hair. 'No, they're very much around…we're just not close.'

'How come?' He couldn't understand it. The way she'd handled Lily, the love she had for the sister she'd lost, he'd expected them to be close. He certainly hadn't expected to put her on edge. And though he wanted the blush back in her cheeks, the fire in her eyes, the laughter, he wanted to understand more.

'We drifted apart when…when Amy died.'

She lowered her eyes to her lap, to where her hands now were, and he knew she twisted them together just as she had in the car.

He reached across the table, his hand resting beside her wine glass, and her eyes came back to him.

'They must miss you,' he said. 'I can't imagine losing Lily, to know that she is somewhere in the world and not be close to her.'

'I'm not sure.' She looked back to her hands as she paused. 'I think I'm a constant reminder of what they lost.'

He shook his head, but she wasn't looking at him.

'We don't really talk. We used to, before… Everything was different then, but after… I just couldn't face them, I didn't want to see the blame in their eyes, you know.' She gave a shrug and looked to him, her tormented gaze tugging at him.

'They wouldn't have blamed you,' he said softly.

She gave a shake of her head and reached out for her wine glass. 'It's how it felt. It was far easier to stay out of their way.'

'And so you locked yourself away?'

'Pretty much. Now it's just the norm.'

'Don't you have any other brothers, sisters?'

'No. Just me.'

Her voice was strained. His own, low and husky as he asked, 'Is that why you work so hard?'

Her eyes flicked to his, a surprising smile playing about her lips. 'Are you psychoanalysing me, Jack?'

His chest tightened. 'I guess I am.'

She shook her head some more, her smile indulging him. 'I have a need to prove myself, to succeed, to make my life worthy, if the therapist in you needs to know…' She looked away from him and her smile fell, her voice turning distant. 'I was the one who survived after all. I owe it to Amy to achieve.'

'There's achievement and then there's happiness, Sophia.' He pulled her attention back to him, his eyes searching hers and looking for the truth. 'Are you happy?'

She shrugged but he knew it was a front for what was really happening beneath the surface, behind her swirling blues.

'What's not to be happy about?' Her voice was steady, level, defiant. 'I'm the youngest hotel manager Devereaux Leisure has ever seen; I can afford my own apartment in London and I don't need a man or flatmate to do it. There aren't many twenty-four-year-olds who can claim the same.'

'But are you happy?'

He knew the answer; he could read it in her forced nonchalance, the way her fingers shook a little as she raised the glass to her lips and finished her wine.

'I'm happy enough.'

'I think Amy would want you to be happy above all else… Your parents too.'

Her throat bobbed, her eyes glistened, and he

suddenly felt like the worst man in the world to make her suffer. He'd gone too far.

'Okay, Mr Know-It-All,' she suddenly fired at him. 'Tell me, are *you* happy?'

He should have expected it, her turning the tables on him. But he felt no more prepared, no more capable of giving an honest answer. And he didn't need to give one as the bill arrived. He placed his card on the small metal tray without looking, his eyes locked with her probing ones.

And he realised, for the first time in a long time, he did feel a sense of happiness, of being where he belonged, sitting across from a woman who sparked such feelings that he was torn between running for the hills and taking her home. And the latter could only ever end badly. She deserved more than what he could ever give her.

So why aren't you bringing an end to it now? Why aren't you walking away?

He couldn't explain it. It was impulsive—the need to be with her, to get to know her—and impossible to resist.

That realisation should have had him running too. Instead, he was looking into her eyes and telling himself it would be okay. He just had to be careful. Controlled. Sensible.

He ran a billion-pound empire so they were qualities he possessed in spades, and he should be able to rely on them now. But as he continued to lose himself in her gaze, he started to doubt even himself.

'Sir?'

It was the waiter, offering the card machine and judging by the amusement he could spy in Sophia's gaze it wasn't the first time he'd tried to get his attention.

Careful. Controlled. Sensible. Restrained.

He punched in his PIN with each word.

He started to rise. 'Shall we?'

'Good to have you back in the room, Jack.'

Her eyes sparkled with her teasing, her humour reaching right inside him and warming him through, pushing out the panic, the worry, the warning sounds in his head.

He offered his hand to her and she slipped her fingers into his, getting to her feet, all the while her eyes locked with his.

She was beautiful, she was funny and, without thinking any further, he leant in, his mouth brushing beside her ear. 'You make me feel happy.'

CHAPTER FIVE

AS THEY STEPPED out into the brisk winter's night Sophia shivered. Not from the chilling wind that whipped around them, but from the memory of his touch against her ear. It had hardly been there at all—just the brush of his lips. But the power of it…

'Are you cold?' He frowned down at her, clearly spying the tremor and misreading its cause. 'Maybe a walk isn't such a great idea.'

'No, no, it would be nice to get some fresh air. I don't make enough time for it these days.' She pulled her thick woollen coat tightly around her and smiled up at him. 'But if you want to wuss out?'

He grinned, his arm hooking around her waist and setting off a new string of fireworks inside.

'No way.'

Was he as surprised as she at the protective gesture? If he was, he didn't make any show of it. Instead, they walked in step with one another, completely at ease as though they'd been doing it for years, when in reality she'd never walked like this before, a man's arm around her.

She bowed her head against the wind and the odd spot of rain starting to fall, her thoughts turning to his late wife and whether this was something they had done often. Maybe even the exact same thing, dining at the same restaurant, taking a walk around Hyde Park after?

A multitude of scenarios played out in her head, her internet search having provided the perfect image of Elena and their projected happiness together. Her heart panged inside her chest and she hunched her shoulders, fending it off.

'What are you thinking about?'

She felt his eyes burning down into her, but she couldn't look at him, couldn't tell him the honest answer either.

'Sophia?'

Her softly spoken name tugged at her and she found herself looking up at him, forcing a smile. 'I guess you don't get to do this often either?'

'What, take a walk?'

'Yes.'

'I do, as it happens. Lily and I take a walk every Saturday morning, even in the rain.'

She grinned. 'Ah, muddy puddle days.'

'Indeed.' His eyes narrowed on her. 'You know, for someone who doesn't have children, you sure know what they like.'

'My friend Samantha has a five-year-old boy. I

figure mud is just as appealing at that age whether you're a boy or a girl. Nothing beats donning wellies and making the most of the puddles.'

He laughed, the deep rumble working its way through her. 'Don't tell Lily that; she'll be dragging you outside in all your hotel finery, wellies or not.'

She laughed too, the joyful image he painted coming alive in her brain. 'Any time.'

'Any time?' he repeated, clearly not believing she was serious.

A smile continued to tease at her lips, the idea of doing exactly that with both Lily and him far too appealing. Appealing and just as unrealistic. Her breath stuttered in her chest and it took her a second to recover.

'Don't look so surprised about it, Jack,' she murmured when she could. 'I'm not afraid of a little mud.'

No, she was more afraid of enjoying their company a little too much.

He pursed his lips and nodded. 'Or crawling underneath tables to play hide-and-seek with my daughter...'

In spite of her unsettled thoughts, she laughed some more. 'She was actually star-gazing.'

'With her torch?'

'I take it you've done that with her before?'

'She's a little obsessed.'

'There are plenty worse things she could be

obsessed with. Take slime, for example; it gets *everywhere*.'

'Oh, no, we've been there too. You should have seen the clean-up fee they charged on my last hotel suite.'

Her eyes snapped to his. 'Am I to expect the same?'

'Oh, dear…' He cringed, his boyish hesitation tickling at her. 'I'd forgotten who you were for a second.'

She had too. She wanted to be someone different; she wanted to be the kind of woman who would date someone like Jack.

He stopped walking, encouraging her to do the same. 'Forget I mentioned it?'

'That depends…what's it worth?'

His eyes darkened, his hands lifting to cup her upper arms and hold her still. The wind, the rain, the passers-by, all fell away. 'Name your price.'

Price. She'd asked for that and her cheeks warmed against the cold night air while her mind seared with her answer: *a kiss.*

It was written in her face, in her eyes, she was sure. But she had no right to ask for such a gesture, no right to even think it. It was foolish and… no, she couldn't.

She turned back towards his car. 'The rain is picking up; we should head back.'

He was slower to follow, as if he too had been caught in the same momentary fairy tale, but then he was there, his arm back around her waist, bringing his warmth and his comforting presence.

But they'd had their meal, the night would be over soon and tomorrow both Jack and Lily would be back to being just guests in her hotel. The sooner she accepted that, the sooner she could protect herself from getting too attached.

Don't you think it's a little late for that already?

'So, what do you say, Sophia?' Jack said into the sudden quiet, and lustful heat wedged its way into her throat. He wanted to know her price...

'Will you have another dinner with Lily and me?'

Phew. No, not phew. She went from overheated to cold and back to overheated in a heartbeat. Another dinner was worse than some flirtatious demand. Wasn't it?

She gave him a quick look, saw the wish for her to say yes in his imploring greys, and lowered her eyes back to the path.

You can't say yes. He's your hotel guest. You're attached enough already.

But she couldn't say no either.

She *wanted* that time with them both. For however long they were in her life, she wanted to enjoy it. And if that meant one more meal, then one more meal it would be.

'Yes.'

'Tomorrow?'

'Tomorrow?' She sounded breathless, her pulse

racing with a strange mix of excitement and trepidation. 'So soon?'

'You really don't know Lily if you think she'll wait a day more.'

She gave an anxious laugh. He had a point. And doing it tomorrow meant less time to panic in the meantime. 'Okay…tomorrow it is.'

'Great!'

His grin made every anxious flicker worth it. She wanted to make him happy. She wanted to make Lily happy. And if it made her happy too…

'Are you sure it's just Lily who's impatient?' she teased, hooking her arm through his.

'What can I say? She has as many of my traits as her mother's.'

He didn't pale or tense up over the mention of Elena and she took the change to be a good sign, an encouraging one.

'So, aside from impatience, what else does she get from you?'

He gave another laugh. 'Stubbornness, a dictatorial manner, and she's frustratingly independent, messy…'

'Wow—please tell me her mother gave her some softer qualities, else you'll have a monster on your hands when she hits her teens.' She was purposely light and teasing with it, but she wanted to know more about Elena. More about the woman who had secured his love so completely and given him a beautiful daughter.

His laugh was soft, reflective. 'Luckily she does.'

'Like?' she pressed gently.

'Her mother's heart for one, her carefree spirit, impulsiveness, sparkle obsession… The list goes on.'

She smiled at the ease with which the details flowed from him now. 'It's an interesting mix.'

His murmured agreement came from deep within his chest.

'You must miss her…' she said quietly, giving his arm a squeeze and looking up at him. 'Elena?'

He met her eye briefly and there was so much in that one look, but she couldn't label it. It wasn't grief, it wasn't pain… It looked more…bewildered, uncertain. 'We knew each other a long time.'

That was an interesting way to put it. 'How did you two meet?'

He turned away, his eyes on the passing cars now as he went quiet. So much for her not wanting to bring back his pain. 'Sorry, you don't need to talk about her with me. I shouldn't pry.'

He surprised her with a laugh as he stopped walking and shook his head at her. 'After all I've prised out of you tonight, that hardly seems fair.'

Her laugh was awkward as she realised the truth of it. 'Fair point. You did get my life story—which has been untold until now, I might add. But still, it's okay if you don't want to.'

He studied her for a moment, searching her gaze, and she wondered again if he was surprised by their behaviour. Not only in their actions but their honesty too. She almost asked when he started to walk again, taking her with him.

'We were placed in the same foster home when we were thirteen,' he eventually said.

'Thirteen?' Her heart pulsed; they'd known each other for ever... 'You were both so young.'

'Yes.' His eyes stayed fixed on the road. 'She'd been in care for nearly as long as me.'

'Did neither of you get adopted?'

'No,' he scoffed gently. 'At first there was hope that I'd return home to my mother and Elena to her parents, but it never happened.'

'I'm so sorry.'

He shrugged. 'They had their reasons and then my mother was no longer around, so it wasn't an option.'

She couldn't bring herself to admit that she'd read about his mother, but he likely knew it anyway.

'What about Elena's parents?'

'Her father's in prison, as far as I'm aware, and her mother remarried. Last I knew, Isla had a whole other life—kids, family, all of it. Not that Elena ever became a part of that life again. She was an adult by the time her mother had sorted herself out and by then...' His voice trailed off.

'By then she had you?'

He gave her a soft smile but his eyes were sad, haunted. 'Yes.'

'She was lucky to have met you.'

He scoffed at that, his rejection making her frown. How could he even doubt it when he'd so obviously given them both a better life?

'Does Elena's mother see Lily?'

'She saw her once, not long after Lily was born. Elena wanted to try and forge some kind of a relationship. Becoming a mother herself made her realise that it wasn't a bond so easily forgotten, and she hoped Lily would help bring them back together.'

She could hear the bitter ring to his voice and knew that wasn't how it had gone down. 'But it didn't?'

'I think Isla saw Elena as a reminder of a past she wanted to forget. She was still young; she had Elena at fifteen.'

'Fifteen?'

'Far too young, which is why we understood her fear, her difficulty, her avoidance of it all, but…'

'But she still didn't want to know?'

'It wasn't so much that she didn't, I don't think. More that she was torn between her old life and the new. She had a husband by then, two children and another on the way.'

'Poor Elena.' She squeezed his arm tighter. 'It must have been hard seeing her mother so settled with a new family.'

He gave an awkward shrug and she knew he was trying to make light of something that still hurt.

'Isla did come to her funeral, but... I don't know, too little too late, I guess.'

'Does Lily know her?'

'She's knows of her, but she was just a baby when they met. It would be nice if things were different. It's not like Lily has any other grand-parents...'

'Do you think you might try again in the future?'

'Perhaps. It was all too raw at the funeral. She left her number with me and asked me to call but...'

'You haven't got around to it?'

He sighed. 'Is it awful to say I haven't?'

'No, not really.'

'It's not that I haven't thought about it; it's just... how do I know I can trust her to stick around, to let Lily become attached and have her walk away again? I don't want that guilt on my shoulders too.'

'Perhaps you could visit her, talk to her about your concerns. I think you'll know if she's ready to be a part of Lily's life.'

'Maybe...' He glanced down at her, his eyes soft and warm, reeling her in. 'Thank you for this, for understanding and listening.'

'No need to thank me. You've done exactly the same for me.'

'Be that as it may, thank you.'

'Then thank you too.' She smiled up at him, her happiness swelling as they walked ever closer together. 'I really have enjoyed tonight.'

'Me too,' he murmured, and her smile grew.

Ahead, his driver had spied their return and approached them with an umbrella in hand. It reminded her of the rain that had started to fall; it also reminded her of who Jack was outside the happy little fantasy bubble in which she walked. But it didn't burst it, rather it made her smile further because, for a fantasy, she really couldn't write it better than this.

'Thank you,' she said to his driver as he positioned the umbrella over them for the remaining distance to the car.

'You're welcome, ma'am.'

She had to stop the little giggle that wanted to escape. *Ma'am*. Never had she been called that before.

They settled into the back of the car. This time there was barely a hair's breadth between them, and she started to wish she lived further away, that the traffic would be heavier, that the fancy black car would break down– anything to keep her in it for longer. With him.

But, of course, it wasn't to be and as they pulled up outside her apartment she had to ignore the sudden sadness that had the chill of reality setting back in. Of her empty apartment that would greet her and the memories she wouldn't be able to fend off.

'This is me…' she said, stating the obvious but floundering with what she was supposed to do now. What was the etiquette for saying goodbye on a date that wasn't a date?

His driver opened her door and she turned to smile back at Jack.

'Thank you for a lovely evening.' And then, before she could think otherwise, she leaned in and pressed a kiss to his cheek, her body coming alive against the warmth of his. She breathed in deep and pulled back.

'Sophia?' He reached for her hand.

'Hmm?'

His eyes fell briefly to her lips, their depths dark and glittering, and she wondered if he would kiss her. She wet her lips, waiting, wanting, and then he seemed to shake himself out of it. 'Shall we come by and pick you up about ten tomorrow morning?'

'Ten? A bit early for dinner, isn't it?'

'You got me…' His thumb stroked across the back of her hand, the simple caress drawing her eye as the power of it took over her senses. 'I thought I might be able to sneak that under the radar.'

She laughed, the sound high and giddy as she read the reasoning behind his words and couldn't quite believe it. 'As much as I'd love to, I'm working a half day tomorrow…'

'On a Saturday?'

'The hotel doesn't stop just because it's the weekend.'

'Of course.'

'I can get away about two though, if that works for you? Here, take this…' She pulled away to rummage through her bag and took out a scrap of paper and a pen. She quickly wrote down her number and passed it to him. 'Just in case you change your mind, or something comes up.'

He took hold of it, their fingers lightly brushing and neither moving away.

'It would take a sudden blizzard to stop us going out with you, Sophia.'

She found herself tongue-tied and getting drawn into his steely grey eyes that seemed to mirror everything she was feeling. No matter how fantastical that idea was.

'But, luckily for us,' he said, the husky edge to his voice impossible to ignore now, 'we're all in the same building, so not even that excuse will hold.'

She smiled softly. 'So true.'

'I'll meet you in the foyer then? Just after two?'

She nodded.

'See you then, Sophia.'

'Goodnight, Jack.'

His smile was slow as he leaned back into his seat, taking her number with him. ''Night, Sphea.'

She grinned at Lily's name for her and shook

her head, sliding out of the car and thanking his driver too.

She was still smiling as she walked through the foyer, up the flights of stairs and unlocked the door to her apartment. Still smiling ten minutes later when she had a cup of hot cocoa wrapped in her hands and breathed in its rich, comforting scent. And even when she climbed into bed, her mind awash with thoughts of him, her body too alive to sleep.

She'd been worried about the past creeping back in, bringing the sadness with it, but with Jack on her mind there was no room for it.

It wasn't a long-term fix, but she could certainly make the most of it…for now.

CHAPTER SIX

'ARE YOU SURE she's definitely coming, Daddy?'

Jack smiled down at his daughter and retied her tartan scarf for the umpteenth time. 'Definitely— she's just finishing up and then she'll be with us.'

'I hope so.' She looked to the row of wellies at her feet. 'I think we should have bought different colours *and* sizes. What if she doesn't like red?'

'How can she not like red when it's the colour of…' His words fell away as he glanced over his daughter's head to see Sophia enter the hotel foyer, her smile lighting him up inside. She'd changed out of her workwear into jeans and a winter coat ready for their outing, its deep red colour setting off both her hair and her eyes. Stunning didn't even come close. 'Looks like you can ask her yourself, kiddo.'

Lily spun on her heel and gave a little squeal of delight as she ran straight up to her, her dark curls bouncing around her shoulders and her scarf trailing behind once again. 'Sphea!'

Sophia dropped to her haunches, her arms outstretched ready to take the cuddle Lily was reaching out for. She squeezed his little girl to her, her eyes lifting to find him over Lily's shoulder and he felt himself grin. She had only been in Lily's life a couple of days but it seemed like more; he felt something shift inside of him. Something he couldn't latch onto or understand. Then her gaze fell to the row of wellies at his feet and her amused frown tickled him into a laugh.

'We bought you something,' Lily said as Sophia fixed her scarf for her.

'You did?'

Lily nodded and took Sophia's hand as she straightened up. 'Come see.'

She started to drag her along and Sophia looked from Lily to him and back down to the wellies again.

'We went for a few different sizes,' he said, 'but hopefully one of these pairs will fit.'

'You bought me *wellies*?' Her blue eyes sparkled as she looked up at him, her glossy pink lips stretching wide. 'I don't think anyone has bought me wellies before, not since I was a child at any rate.'

'Well, it's not a blizzard out there,' he said, recalling their conversation the night before, 'but it's certainly been raining cats and dogs.'

'Cats and dogs?' Lily frowned. 'That makes no sense, Daddy.'

Sophia laughed. 'You're right, it doesn't, but I still can't believe you've bought me wellies.'

'Well, Daddy said you like muddy puddles too.'

'Did he now?'

He gave a shrug. 'It may have come up in conversation.'

'You need to try them on, Sphea, then Daddy can ask Alice to take the others back.'

'Alice?'

'My PA and general life organiser.'

She smiled. 'You really shouldn't have.'

'Technically, I didn't.'

She shook her head, her eyes wide with some unknown thought, and then she looked at the wellies and to Lily. 'Do you have a size six there?'

'I'll find it,' his daughter declared, pulling out the right pair quicker than he could even say anything.

Not that he knew what to say because every phrase that entered his head seemed too inappropriate and...*gushy*. It was a word he had never used, let alone attributed to himself. And he could be neither of those things, particularly in front of Lily. But he wanted to tell her how lovely she looked, how much they'd been looking forward to this outing, how much—

Stop, just stop.

'Here you go...' Lily lifted the pair of shiny red wellies high above her head. 'The colour matches your hair and Daddy got me a matching pair too!'

'Thank you.' Sophia smiled down at her, her expression so unguarded with affection for Lily. He could be excused for getting wrapped up in that same look, surely. It had nothing to do with him softening towards her, nothing whatsoever.

He'd hardly been soft with Elena, hardly let such emotion in at all until he'd first held Lily in his arms.

'I'll just go and put my shoes away.'

She turned to leave and Lily grabbed her hand. 'Wait!'

Lily bent low and picked up a small bag, offering it out. 'Daddy got you welly socks too!'

'He did?' Sophia's brow lifted, her eyes widening further on another laugh. 'How thoughtful…'

'Sorry if it's too much…' he started but she shook her head.

'No, not at all. I won't be long.'

She was still shaking her head as she returned, her eyes dancing bright and blue as she pulled a knitted beige bobble hat from her pocket and slid it on. 'Let's go before those ominous grey clouds return.'

'Higher, Daddy, higher!' Lily squealed as Jack pushed her on the swing and Sophia watched on.

The play park was relatively quiet—people avoiding the wet equipment, she supposed—but it meant Lily could hop from one thing to the next, no jostling for best position, and she was keeping them both on their toes as she rushed about.

They'd done jumping in puddles, they'd done ice cream in the freezing cold, and they'd made themselves sick on the roundabout and enjoyed the grown-up slide, which had produced waves worthy of a log flume, much to Lily's delight, not so much Jack's. He'd managed to get a shower of it to the face as he waited for her at the bottom, something which had evoked fits of giggles from both Lily and Sophia, and no matter how he'd frowned at them they couldn't quit it.

Even now, Sophia was still grinning and laughing, her cheeks and belly aching from the effort.

It was such a perfect afternoon, perfect and so different to how she'd spent the previous weekend and the weekend before that. Memories of Amy haunted her as they always did this time of year but it was so nice to be out in the fresh air and not be worrying, not be anxious.

She'd known Jack would prove to be a distraction and though she knew he and his daughter were a fleeting presence in her life she couldn't stop herself from taking pleasure in every second.

'Hey, Soph, what are you doing here?'

Oh, God.

She turned to see Samantha, her friend and next-door neighbour, heading towards her, her son Noah scooting along in front, and she felt her cheeks flush.

'Hi, guys!'

She could sense both Jack and Lily watching her and her smile felt forced, her voice too. It was one thing enjoying her time with the McGregors, but it was another to merge her fantasy life with the real.

She embraced Samantha and gave her a kiss to the cheek, ruffling Noah's hair too. 'You've come to enjoy the park?'

'Yeah,' Noah said, his blond hair escaping from beneath his knitted beanie so like his mum's; his grin was wide and showed off the gap in his front teeth.

'Gotta get out while the sun is shining,' Samantha added, her head tilted towards the swings, her eyes wide and gesturing. It was obvious Sophia was with them. Why else would she be standing there watching them like some oddball? She was going to have to introduce them; the alternative was even more awkward. She only had herself to blame too—bringing them to this park, her local park.

She brushed her hands down her coat and took a breath, looking over to Jack and Lily, who were clearly waiting on her to say something. Jack looked mildly curious but Lily looked strangely apprehensive.

'Jack, Lily, come and meet my friends...' she called out, trying to relax her smile and her voice, both of which were supremely difficult with Sam making goo-goo eyes at a grinning Jack. Sophia nudged her subtly in the side, saying between her teeth, 'You're married.'

'Nothing wrong with looking, Soph,' she returned under her breath.

Lily hopped off the swing with a leap but soon shied away behind the legs of her father as they approached, her usual confidence non-existent.

'This is my friend, Samantha, and her son, Noah.'

'Nice to meet you, Samantha.'

Jack held out his hand and her friend was quick to shake it.

'Oh, Sam, please.'

Her friend giggled and the sound had Sophia's cheeks flushing deeper, even more so when Sam's eyes flitted from Jack to Sophia and back again. She was so in for it next time Sam had her alone.

'Jack is a guest at my hotel.'

'A guest, you say?' Sam's voice was drawn out with various other possibilities running rife through her gossip-charged brain.

'Yes,' Jack confirmed as Sophia's brain screamed at her friend to quit whatever she was thinking. 'My Lily has taken quite a shine to her.'

And speaking of Lily, the girl was still hiding behind Jack's legs. Sophia ignored her internal panic and crouched down to the girl's level, wishing to put her at ease. 'Hey, Lily, you and Noah are the same age, you know.'

She edged out just enough to look at Noah beneath her lashes.

'Hi, Lily.' Noah grinned at her, all confident and a total contrast to the shrinking violet Lily had become. 'When's your birthday?'

'The twenty-eighth of February.'

'Oh, cool. Mine's next weekend. You having a party?'

She looked up at her father and Sophia caught the faint grimace on his face.

'I don't know,' she said, her eyes back on Noah.

'Do you want a go on my scooter?' He pushed it out towards her. 'I can show you some tricks if you like?'

She bit her lip and looked from Jack to Sophia, before looking back to Noah. 'I don't think I'd be very good on one.'

'Why not?'

'I've never been on a scooter before.'

Noah's brows disappeared into his hat. 'You're kidding, right?'

Lily turned the colour of her wellies. 'No.'

'Come on, there's a ramp over there—I can show you some moves. Don't worry, I won't make you do it too, not unless you want to… I can help you, if you like?'

'Go easy, Noah, love.' Samantha rested her hand on her son's shoulder. 'Lily's only just met you.'

Noah shrugged, his grin wide and widening further when Lily smiled at him.

'I'd like that.'

'Cool!'

'So long as you have the time, Sam?' Sophia asked her friend, half wishing Sam had some place else to be, because this felt too real, as if Jack could really belong in her world if she let him in.

'Sure we do. Dan's had to pop into the office, a last-minute hiccup with a high profile project; you know that kind of thing.' She rolled her eyes dramatically. 'Best he gets it sorted and then we can at least enjoy tomorrow in peace.'

'Great—thanks, Mum. Come on, Lil!'

Noah started scooting away and Lily looked to her father and then to Sophia. She was nervous, unsure of herself, and Sophia's heart ached for her.

'Noah's good fun, Lily, you'll see,' she encouraged her softly. 'Go on, we're coming too.'

The little girl started off in his direction, glancing back over her shoulder twice just to be sure they followed and then she was fully focused on Noah as he whooped his way around the ramps, her shyness gradually falling away as he called out to her and involved her.

It was strange to see Lily stripped of her confidence. She glanced at Jack as they followed them across the park and though he watched his daughter there was no indication he thought anything amiss…unless she recalled the grimace he'd given when the birthday party had been mentioned.

Sophia would hazard a guess that the answer to the birthday party question was a no. No party. No celebration with kids of her own age. And though she knew he meant well, would he see that Lily was actually missing out on things that were considered a normal part of growing up?

A real childhood, with playdates, friends, fun and laughter.

She didn't doubt how happy Lily was with her father, but she couldn't ignore the fact that the little girl was missing out on playing with children her own age. Her shyness with Noah a sad result of it.

'So how long are you staying for then, Jack?'

Sophia pulled herself out of her thoughts at Samantha's conversation starter. She needed to keep her wits about her. She wouldn't put it past her friend to say something completely inappropriate that would have Jack wishing for the ground to open up and swallow him whole. Or, worse, running in the opposite direction and taking his dear, sweet Lily with him.

It was an outcome she should perhaps be grateful for, but it wasn't gratitude that made her chest ache at the idea.

The Italian Jack had chosen for dinner that evening was bustling, but his request to add two to the reservation had only resulted in a twenty-minute delay and the kids had decided the extra time would be perfect for sampling milkshakes at the bar.

Even now they were thick as thieves, laughing about something as they sucked on their straws, barely coming up for air. Quite a change from the Lily who had hidden behind his legs at the park…

'This really is very kind of you both, letting us gatecrash like this,' Samantha was saying. 'I think Noah had resigned himself to a day with just me and him.'

'Nothing wrong with that,' Sophia told her. 'Mother-and-son time is awesome too.'

Samantha twirled her straw in the mojito she'd opted for, her face losing some of its exuberance. 'I'm not so sure. Not when it's becoming routine that Dan has to work Saturday and miss out on his footie practice.' She gave a little sigh but then smiled. 'Still, he's promised to make up for it tomorrow and that's better than not at all.'

'Well, his loss is our gain,' Sophia said, gently shoulder barging her friend. 'And in the meantime you get to enjoy our scintillating company and pizza.'

'That's true.' Samantha gave her a grin and looked back to the two kids who sat opposite each other, leaning forward so that their heads were practically glued together as they talked. 'I think Noah's certainly found a firm friend there; just a shame you're not stopping longer, Jack.'

He felt that same weird tightness in his chest,

a sense that the sand was flowing too quickly through the hourglass, but he masked it all with a smile. 'We'll be back in London at some point... We'll have to keep in touch.'

He looked to Sophia. Would they keep in touch too? And what did he really hope to achieve by doing that?

'Mum!' Noah suddenly turned to them. 'Can Lily come to my party on Saturday?'

Samantha looked to Jack. 'She's more than welcome. He's just having a few friends over to play some party games and eat far too many E numbers to count.'

'She's not lying about the E numbers,' Sophia warned him. 'Choose wisely.'

He laughed as Lily pleaded, '*Please*, Daddy!'

'Okay, okay, I don't see why not.'

Sophia and Samantha both smiled at him.

'What can I say—she has me wrapped around her little finger.'

'Nothing wrong with that, Jack,' Samantha said, nodding her approval.

'No, nothing at all.' Sophia's voice had a softness to it, kind of wistful. He caught her eye and she quickly shifted her attention to Samantha and party preparations, food and things that Jack really knew little about.

He *was* a good father now. He knew he was— he put Lily first in everything. But party planning, kids' get-togethers, games...there he was lacking.

And did that mean Lily was too?

He spent the rest of the meal listening to both sides of the table, mentally taking notes and accepting that perhaps it was time for a change. He just had no idea where to start.

He was still pondering it long after they'd taken Sam and Noah home, Sophia heading back to the hotel with them, thanks to a pleading Lily who wanted a bedtime story. Not from him, but from her.

The alarm bells were starting to ring in earnest. How long could they keep up the association before Lily became attached? And if she did become attached, what did that mean for the future?

He approached Lily's door, his bare feet quiet on the marble floor, and listened. He could hear Sophia's soft, dulcet tones as she read from Lily's latest book, felt the soothing effect of her voice over himself too and he no longer questioned his daughter's choice. Given the option, he'd opt for Sophia to read to him too.

He reached the gap in the door and stilled; his heart caught in his chest. Sophia was in his place, fulfilling the role he had done almost every night for the last three years. She was lying on Lily's bed, her arm hooked around Lily, Baby Bear tucked between them as she read.

He dropped back a little, wanting to remain inconspicuous, wanting nothing to disturb the perfect scene before him. He could see Lily was drifting off, her eyes slowly closing before snapping wide again. She was doing her best to stay awake, but tiredness was winning out. And Sophia was doting on her. Every now and then she'd nuzzle into Lily and place a kiss to her brow, stroke her hair or brush it from her eyes. They looked so perfect together, so…normal.

He told himself it was because he wasn't used to it. That it had been so long since he'd witnessed anyone else in this role.

He told himself it had nothing to do with his feelings towards Sophia.

He also told himself he was a liar.

He settled against the doorframe and just watched, a slight smile lifting his lips as he let the vision work its magic over him. He couldn't deny that a part of him wished this was the norm. That Lily had a mother and he had a wife, and all was merry and bright.

Only he knew the truth of it. Life wasn't like that. It wasn't all roses and happily ever afters.

He worked hard to be able to provide for his daughter; he worked hard to ensure that money was never an obstacle, but he couldn't control life outside of that.

And he couldn't control his heart either. He wasn't capable of loving another like they deserved to be loved. He could love Lily, he could be there for Lily, but over and above that…no.

He'd tried once with Elena and failed.

He'd witnessed too many failed marriages before that too, lived with too many messed-up kids who were the unlucky result of such marriages and he had no interest in exposing Lily to that kind of life. It was safer just the two of them; there was less that could go wrong, fewer variables at play.

And now you sound like you're talking about a business deal...

But then he had a head for business. He'd promised Elena, sworn on her dead body, that he would do everything to make amends for what he'd done. That he would keep Lily safe, he would love her and cherish her, and be there for her. He had no room in his life for more, for someone as beautiful and enchanting as the woman now cuddling his sleeping child in her arms.

A weight settled in his gut as he pushed himself off the doorframe and made his presence known, realising as Sophia caught his eye that, regardless of his promise and all that he had sworn to live by, a small part of him wished things could be different.

It was the same part that wasn't ready to let Sophia out of their lives just yet.

'Hi,' he whispered.

'Has she gone?'

He nodded, his smile filled with the warmth persisting in spite of his mental turmoil. 'I'll help you.'

He crossed the room and leaned over the bed, lifting Lily's heavy head from Sophia's arm so that she could slip out. He laid his daughter back down and Sophia pulled the quilt higher up her body, tucking it beneath her chin. He leaned in to kiss his daughter's head and ended up being head to head with Sophia as she'd gone to do the same. Their eyes collided and in that one look he saw so much, felt so much deep inside.

His eyes fell to her lips, the urge to kiss her so natural and strong that he was lucky she pulled back, lucky she'd seen sense where he couldn't.

He kissed his daughter's forehead and straightened up, reminding himself of the promises he'd made and why.

Only the reasoning was starting to feel woolly, less reasonable…bordering on monastic even.

Sophia padded out of the room, a move he sensed rather than saw as his eyes were fixed on his daughter, his mind focused on the reasoning that had always seemed so solid.

He already felt so much for Sophia, so much that he could hardly get a handle on it, and though he was sure it had a lot to do with Lily's feelings for her, it didn't help.

Maybe they just needed to agree on expectations now to avoid any future confusion. Set some ground rules even. Chaos at work was the result of mismanagement, so maybe he just needed to lay down the law in his personal life and protect both Lily and Sophia.

Who was he kidding? He wanted to protect himself too.

It had been harrowing losing Elena, a woman for whom he'd cared deeply but hadn't loved as she'd wanted, as she'd deserved. He was convinced he was wired wrong, that being stuck in the system for so long had screwed him up emotionally. Even Elena had thrown as much at him on many occasions; virtually every fight had come down to his inability to care, to think of her enough, to empathise.

And he'd come to believe she was right, but now he wasn't so sure. Whatever Sophia sparked in him, it was new and it was different, and it scared him half to death.

But not enough to run the other way…

CHAPTER SEVEN

'YOU REALLY ARE a natural.'

Sophia looked up at the sound of Jack's voice and felt her cheeks colour, as if she'd been caught doing something she shouldn't. But she was only guilty of curling up on the L-shaped sofa that dominated the living area in his penthouse suite.

This wasn't her domain though. As much as she knew this suite like she knew her own home, she didn't belong, not like this.

But she felt as if she did.

She'd felt it when she'd been lying next to Lily, reading her the story. She'd felt it all day as they'd laughed and joked and enjoyed the company of her friends. And she felt it now… It was only the rational side of her brain telling her it was all still fantasy.

'A natural?' She cocked a brow and let her eyes fall to the empty glasses hooked in his fingers and the bottle of red he carried—the very rare bottle of red that would have been pulled out of the cellar especially. *Definitely* all fantasy.

He offered her a glass and she took it, wetting her lips. She shouldn't be taking it; she shouldn't be letting this evening continue now Lily was asleep. But the sound of the deep red liquid hitting the glass told her otherwise. Her tummy fluttered with a mixture of nerves and desire...

But she did want to talk to him about Lily, and it was as good a reason as any to stay longer.

Still, she wasn't fool enough to think it was her only reason.

'You're a natural with kids, with Lily,' he explained as he poured his own glass and set the bottle down on the large glass coffee table. 'You looked completely at home reading her a story.'

He joined her on the sofa—not close enough that she could feel the sofa dip but close enough that her entire body came alive with awareness of his.

She took a sip of the wine and used its soothing warmth to unblock her throat and calm the flutters taking off inside. She felt unbearably hot and cursed her own stupidity for lighting the gas fire that ran along one wall. She hadn't been able to resist it though; it was her favourite feature in the immense suite, that and the view. And she had been cold before his arrival, cold and on edge about the tough conversation she wanted to have and no idea how to broach it.

'I used to read to my sister,' she murmured, her

eyes lost in the flames as she divulged an honest piece of herself and remembered happier times.

'Mum and Dad worked long hours so I'd often take over the bedtime routine—bath, teeth, bed and book.' She risked a glance his way and became transfixed. The grey of his eyes, warmed by the glow of the fire, shone as the pulse in his jaw ticked, his face oddly tense.

She wet her lips. 'Sorry to take your place tonight.'

He shook his head. 'You think that worries me?'

His voice was husky, laced with some emotion that she couldn't quite place. No, she could; she just didn't want to because it suggested he cared and the idea of that only led them down a scary, unknown path.

She smiled tentatively and gave a small shrug. 'I'm not sure.'

He took a breath, his eyes falling to his glass. 'No, it's nice that she wants you to read to her. What…' His eyes came back to her, soft, concerned. 'What bothers me is your relationship with your family. You miss them.'

She was so surprised by his turn in focus that she didn't know how to react, let alone what to say. She shook her head.

'You do, Sophia; it's written in your face when you talk of them. You're so haunted by her loss that you'd rather avoid them than try to forge a relationship of any sort.' He paused, his eyes scanning her face. 'I know I shouldn't compare, but it would kill me to lose touch with Lily, and I think it's slowly eating away at you too.'

'Yes, but I don't know how to fix things. I don't even know where to begin…'

'You just need to be honest with them, talk to them. Yes, it'll be different to how it was, but a new relationship is better than none. And you need to do it while you still can, while they're still around.' He shifted closer, adding quietly, 'We both know how short life can be.'

She took a shaky breath. She knew he was right, knew it and yet she hadn't been able to make that first move. And her parents… Well, they'd given up making the first move long ago.

'It wasn't your fault, Sophia.'

His voice rasped with emotion, its rough edge working over her body like a caress and a hug in one. She felt the spike of tears, felt her throat close and tried to swallow, but it was no use; they were coming and there was nothing she could do about it.

This wasn't what she wanted. She wanted to talk about Lily; she wanted to make him realise that his daughter needed to be around other children, not have some ad hoc therapy session with the man she could so easily fall for…fall for and never have…

She pressed her trembling fingers to her lips

and tried to nod her head in response, to let him know his words had hit home. She felt his arm slip behind her, the warmth of his body as they came together, and she didn't know whether she leaned in or if he'd moved, but she was in his arms, her head tucked beneath his, her body shaking as she let go.

'She was in my care though; she was my responsibility.'

'And you were no more than a child yourself.'

'I was old enough to take care of her and… and…' She couldn't finish it; the tears were too much, the sob shuddering up through her. 'I'm sorry.'

'Please, you don't need to be strong with me, Soph. It's okay to let go.'

She gave a scoff. Strong? It was hardly how she saw herself.

He leaned away to place his glass on the side, came back to take hers next and then his arms were around her and she couldn't pull away. She was too comfortable, too soothed, too lost in his scent and inviting warmth.

'I'm sorry I've upset you, but I couldn't let you leave tonight without saying something. Blame it on me being a father: Lily will never know her mother. Yes, she has a picture by her bed. Yes, I talk about her, what she liked, what they did together…but she'll never have real memories of

her, she'll never know her for herself. She has me
and I'll do all I can to be enough.'

I'll do all I can to be enough...

She took a deep breath, his words hitting so
close to what she wanted to discuss that she
needed to regain her control, to make him see.

'You're a good father.'

He gave a gentle laugh, the move making her
head lift against his chest.

'You *are*...' she insisted.

'But? Why do I sense there's going to be a but?'

She pressed herself off his chest to look at him,
needing him to see that what came next wasn't
designed to hurt him or criticise him; she just
wanted him to see the truth. 'But Lily needs more
than just you.'

His eyes narrowed as his body tensed beneath
her fingers. 'Look, Sophia, I know things between us...between us are... I don't know what
they are...but I have no place in my life for a
woman, for a rel—'

'That's not what I meant,' she choked out, shuf-
fling back on the sofa as she swept her fingers
over her damp cheeks and felt them burn and pale
in an instant.

'It isn't?'

She shook her head, wondering how he could
look disappointed as well as flummoxed when
he'd been midway through lecturing her on how
they could never be. She knew that well enough

on her own. The last thing she needed was to hear him state it in black and white.

He raked his fingers through his hair and blew out a breath. 'Of course. Sorry, I just assumed.'

'Well, you can take your assumption and shove it where—' She pursed her lips tight, her eyes wide in horror at her own outburst. She couldn't remember the last time she'd lost it quite so badly, but then she couldn't remember ever being as embarrassed as she was right now. 'Just because you're used to women willing to hop into bed with you doesn't mean you can count me amongst them.'

Well…he could but he would never know that. 'Is that really what you think?'

'It's not what I think; it's what I know. I'm not about to follow suit.'

'I wasn't referring to *your* lack of desire for me.'

Oh, God, even the word *desire* from his lips had the heat pooling in her lower belly. She straightened her spine, lifted her chin. 'No?'

'No, I was referring to the fact you think women in general are—how did you phrase it?—*willing to hop into bed* with me?'

She could feel her cheeks re-colouring, the warmth whipping through her limbs. This was dangerous territory and so far from the conversation she actually wanted to have.

'If that truly is what you think…' he murmured, low, teasing, his eyes probing hers and reading far too much; he was too near, his body still too close despite the distance she had created '… I find it interesting that you declare yourself…immune.'

Immune!

She was so far from immune it was laughable. And now wasn't the time to laugh. Now was the time to run. But not until she'd spoken to him about Lily.

'So…are you, Sophia?'

'Am I what?' she said, breathless, unblinking, immobile.

'Are you immune to me?'

Jack raked his eyes over her. From her over-bright eyes, drowned out by her pupils, the freed strands of her auburn hair framing her flushed cheeks, her lips parted with the denial she couldn't quite utter. To her soft woollen jumper and denim-clad legs curled beneath her upon the sofa and hiding her fluffy-socked feet—socks *he* had bought her, a first—and *never* had he desired a woman more.

He didn't need skimpy lingerie, fancy dresses, heels, or make-up. He simply needed her. Like this: honest, vulnerable, open. He was captivated. And it meant he should be ending this conversation, not encouraging it.

But could he let it go…?

'Are you, Sophia?' *No, he couldn't.*

She wet her lips. 'You can't ask me that.'

Even her voice turned him on, her words emerging all breathy and heated.

'I think it's good to know where we stand.'

She wet her lips again and his restraint almost snapped. He wanted to taste those lips, wanted to hear her confess that she wanted him, that she wanted him like he did her.

'It doesn't matter whether I want you; in a week you will be gone and that will be that.'

'Be that as it may, it doesn't mean we have to deny it.'

Her eyes flared and his entire body tingled with the need to reach for her. To stroke her cheeks, feel their heat beneath his palms, feel that pulse point at her throat tick beneath his fingertips. He reached for his glass, desperate, needing to keep his hands busy, needing to take a second.

As he drank his wine she watched him, the air fizzing with the unspoken and all the things they could be doing. Her body was so still that if it wasn't for the faint sound of her breathing, the movement of her chest, he'd think she'd turned to stone.

'What are you saying, Jack?'

Her question was as quiet as his glass touching down on the polished surface and as he leaned back he turned into her, close enough that their knees brushed. He didn't miss her sudden intake of breath as the contact zipped through her, just as it did him.

'I'm saying that I want you, Sophia.'

'Jack…' another whisper, accompanied by the tiny shake of her head '…we can't. You even said it just now.'

'I said I didn't have time or, rather, the place in my life for a relationship,' he expanded. 'And the truth is I could never be the man for you, Sophia. You deserve to be loved.' His eyes lingered over her face, taking in all that he had come to…come to what? Come to feel something for? To desire? *No.* It wasn't all desire, but it couldn't be what she would want it to be, what she would need. 'You deserve to be put on a pedestal and adored by a man worthy of you and, as much as I would like to be that man, I know I'm not.'

'How can you know that?'

'Because I've been married, I've been loved and…' He shook his head, the sadness over-whelming. How could he tell her that he hadn't been able to love Elena back in the way that she deserved? Lily's mother, of all people. How could he tell Sophia the cold-hearted truth of how he'd failed her?

'I know I could never take Elena's place,' she said and he could see his own sadness reflected back at him. 'I wouldn't want to.'

'You don't understand, Sophia.'

'What don't I understand?'

'I never *loved* Elena.' His chest tightened, his heart crushed within it, and he saw the second his words hit home, the sudden change to her pallor, the tremble to her lips. 'Not in that way.'

'Of course you did. You looked out for her, you worked hard to make a life for you both, you made Lily, you married her…' She floundered, refusing to accept it.

'I cared for her deeply and I wanted to protect her. I wanted to save her from the life we'd found ourselves in. But I wasn't *in* love with her. I couldn't return her love in the same all-consuming way she loved me. I was devastated when she died—devastated that she'd been taken so young, that she would never see our daughter grow up, that she had died miserable and alone because of me.'

The guilt clawed at him now, the chill pushing out the illicit heat of seconds before.

'I'm sure that's not true.'

'It is.' He hardened his voice and his stance now. 'I'm not a good man, Sophia. I'm not a man you can fall in love with, I'm not a man you should invest your time in. I love that you have brought so much joy to Lily, that she's had this time with you and your friends. But you and I, we can never have a future.'

'You *are* a good man, Jack,' she whispered. 'I know we can't have a future; I understand that. I'd be a fool to think otherwise. But all these things you're saying to me, they're not true. I can't believe them—I won't.'

'Elena did. She believed them through and through, and she would know. She knew me for fourteen years and the last words I had from her were thrown at my answerphone. If I hadn't deleted them I could play them for you now, then maybe you'd believe me.'

She shook her head, the tears returning to her eyes and he knew they were born of sympathy, of pity, and he deserved neither.

'She called me a cold, heartless bastard, and said that if I loved my work so much I could forget coming home, that night or any other for that matter.'

She flung her hand to her lips, but her gasp beneath her fingers was still audible, the shake of her head more severe. 'You can't believe that… you can't.'

'Oh, I believe it all right. If not for the accident, if she hadn't died, she would have left eventually.' He threw back more wine and felt the bitterness, the sadness crawling through him. 'Because she was right. I didn't deserve her. I didn't deserve either of them, and then fate played its hand…' He shook his head. 'Elena never deserved that.'

His body shook, his lungs struggling to take in air. He hadn't cried. Not even when the news had been delivered. Not even that first night back in the empty house when he'd cleared away the untouched dinner. Not even at the funeral. It had all been confirmation that Elena was right. He had no heart and he was incapable of love, bar that which he felt for his daughter.

He was so lost in the rising grief he didn't sense Sophia move, not until her arms were wrapped around him offering the comfort he had so willingly offered her when she'd spoken of her sister. But she deserved it. He didn't.

He pushed himself up off the sofa and out of her hold. He raked his hand over his face and clenched his jaw as he fought back the wave of tears. *Tears!*

'I don't deserve your comfort or your sympathy, Sophia,' he bit out. 'She was right. I didn't love her, but I do love Lily and I will do right by my daughter. I will always do right by her. Outside of that…' he looked down at her, his eyes pleading with her to see the truth '… I can't.'

She stood up slowly, her eyes not leaving his. 'I'm not asking you to give me anything, Jack. No promises, nothing.'

He could believe her as he looked into her eyes and saw her sincerity for what it was. She reached up her hands and cupped his jaw, soft and soothing.

'Truth is, Jack, I've never wanted a man, never wanted to kiss a man, not like I do you.'

'And you shouldn't.'

'But I do…' Her eyes lowered to his mouth and returned twice as fierce, twice as needy. 'I want you to kiss me, Jack.'

'But I—'

'I don't want more…' She stroked one hand back, her fingers tantalisingly soft in his hair. 'I want to be there for you now, in this second. I want you to realise you are worthy of more than you know, I want…'

Her lips brushed over his, finishing the sentence for her, and he couldn't hold back any more. He wrapped his arms around her, pulling her tightly to him. His head slanted to take more of her kiss, to swallow up the blissful moan she released, his own groan just as powerful, just as needy.

He couldn't remember ever feeling more alive, more out of control. It was heady, intense, scary. He dragged his mouth away, her name leaving him on a pained whisper, and then he kissed her harder, his hold tighter. He needed her to be sure, to know what she was taking on.

'Please, Jack, I want this.'

He found her lips again, his tongue feasting inside, teasing at her own. He felt the shiver that ran down her spine beneath his fingers, felt the way she curved her hips against him, and he didn't doubt her, not for a second.

'Even if we only do this once,' she said against his mouth, 'I want you to be my first.'

My first…

He jumped back as though burned, dragging in a lungful of air.

She was a *virgin*.

Their conversation over dinner that first time…
She'd never, not once…?

He'd been Elena's one and only. To be Sophia's
too… His gut lurched as he spun away from all
her flushed glory. How could he?

*Because you're a cold, heartless bastard, that's
how.*

'You need to go, Sophia.'

'But… Jack?'

'Now, Sophia, just go!'

*Before I pull you back to me and take all that
you are offering without a backward glance.*

*Before I ruin what's left of my soul and yours
with it.*

*Before history repeats itself and this time Lily
will witness it all and realise what a failure her
father truly is.*

There was silence behind him. She hadn't
moved and this time he looked at her, projecting all the hardness and self-loathing he could.
'Please, just go.'

She blinked once, twice, then shook her head
and scrubbed her heated cheeks. 'You know what,
Jack, maybe Elena was right. You have no heart,
none at all.'

And then she was gone, her words pulling him
apart inside. It was all he deserved and more.

But it didn't make it easier to bear. It didn't stop
him wanting to run after her and plead for her for-

giveness, to wish that life could be different, that he could be different.

He picked up his wine glass and necked the remainder before pouring another. He stared into the ruby-red liquid as though it possessed all the answers and felt the cold settle around him, inside him.

He was alone, very much alone, and he'd never felt more so.

CHAPTER EIGHT

SOPHIA WAS AVOIDING HIM. He knew it and she knew it.

She'd managed to prevent any chance meeting in the foyer all week by avoiding it all together. She'd not returned any of the missed calls and messages he'd left and the closest they'd got to any interaction had been a note she'd left at Reception for him with the details for Noah's party. Today's party.

Heaven help her...

If only she could have backed out of going, feigned illness, or told Jack that he wasn't welcome. But she couldn't lie, and she wouldn't let her messed-up love life get in the way of Lily enjoying this time with the other kids.

She stared at Sam's inviting lilac door with its ornate yellow frame just like the one out of *Friends* and took a deep breath. It would be fine. There would be no scene, not in front of the children, and with any luck he would have dropped Lily off and fled.

All perfectly fine.

She rapped her knuckles on the door and tried to stop the near constant playback from starting up again in her brain.

With the devastating realisation that he was more tormented by Elena's death than she had ever thought possible came the fact that she cared more than she should. That even though they'd barely met, she'd already been reeled in so completely. And though he claimed he was incapable of having one, he was suffering with a broken heart. One that had been well and truly trodden on by the words Elena had thrown at him in a fit of anger.

And she didn't blame the poor woman. She'd learned enough from Jack to understand the kind of man he was. She knew work would have filled his days and most likely his nights too. But he had done it because he cared, because he *did* have a heart, and he absolutely *did* love.

She also knew she had to apologise to him. She'd lashed out, her words callous and unkind, but then she'd not been thinking clearly. She'd been so hurt by his rejection, embarrassed by her confession that she wanted him to be her first, only to have him reject her. It had crushed her. Made her feel foolish and stupid.

It wasn't until she'd slept on it and replayed it all that she'd understood he'd done it out of concern for her; he'd done it out of the goodness of his heart, not the lack of one.

She shuddered even now as she remembered the whole scene, wishing she'd never divulged that secret. It hadn't been easy to tell him the first time around, and having him label her as too naïve, too innocent to be...to be what? *Defiled* by him.

Maybe if she hadn't been so honest things would be different now. Maybe they'd have made love all night and every night since. Maybe they'd have made a pact to spend every spare private moment together, entwined like the images her dreams taunted her with.

She felt her cheeks colour and her body respond to the idea, and of course the door was opened at that precise moment.

'Sam, I'm so sorry— *Jack!*'

She squeaked and gulped, the sight of the man before her colliding with the naked one still rampant in her heated thoughts.

'Hi...sorry. Samantha has her hands full with the rabble so I said I would get it.'

'You did?' she blurted.

'I figured it would be you since everyone else is here. The kids that is; all the parents have dropped and run.'

'And you didn't want to do the same?' *Oh, please, why couldn't you have done the same...?*

'No, I'm not one for just leaving her places.' His frown told her he thought she was crazy to even suggest it. 'She's either with me or the people I employ to take care of her.'

'You're kidding, right?'

His frown deepened. He was just as incredulous as her and she realised too late the error of her words. Of course he wouldn't entrust Lily's care to just anyone. Samantha hadn't earned his trust and neither had she. And it stung, overtaking her thoughts of an apology, the things she had wanted to take back from the other night, replacing it with more anger, more hurt.

'Well, for your information, Jack,' she bit out, 'Lily *is* safe with us, regardless of what you might think to the contrary. Now, if you'll just excuse me...'

She needed to get out of his company before she did something she'd regret, like say something else that she'd need to take back once she'd calmed down. She lifted Noah's present to her chest, an extra barrier between him and her, and made to go past him but he reached out, his hand gentle on her arm.

'Hang on one sec...please.'

She looked down the hallway to the crack in the door through which she could see the kids playing and hear their excited chatter as they talked over one another and the music that played in the background.

'What is it, Jack? I'm late enough as it is.'

'I didn't just stay for Lily, Sophia.' His voice was soft, ardent, and she could feel her resolve wavering as her gaze met with the warming sincerity of his. 'I wanted to see you.'

She wet her lips. 'You did?'

'I've been trying to all week but…'

She looked away, her cheeks pinking up. 'I know, I just—I just wasn't ready to see you again.'

'I understand that, but I wanted to apologise.'

'Apologise?' She frowned at him. 'Why?'

'Because I shouldn't have backed you into a corner.'

'You didn't—'

'Let me finish. I wasn't fair on you. I just wanted you to understand why.'

'Why what?'

'Why there could never be an us.'

She started to shake her head.

'I didn't do a good job of it,' he continued. 'Of any of it. I didn't want to push you away, but I felt I had to, for your own good, not for mine. Do you understand?'

Understand? Her eyes flared and her body stilled. Of all the patronising, chauvinistic, belittling… She dragged in a breath.

'I understand *perfectly*.' Her eyes darted between the empty outer hallway and the bustling room ahead, wanting no one to hear what came next as she poked him in the chest. 'You used my V plates as reason to reject me. You think I'm not woman enough to take what you're willing to offer and walk away in one piece. Well, I'll have you know, Mr Up-Your-Own-Behind McGregor, I am a woman who knows her own mind, and when I say I want you I mean it.'

His eyes widened with every word, his mouth parting. She'd shocked him. Good.

But now she couldn't tear her eyes from those lips, those tantalisingly full and extremely kiss-able lips, because now she knew how they felt and could remember every last detail.

Her belly fluttered alive, her limbs filling with such lustful warmth she was scared her knees would buckle.

'Just because *you've* lived that little bit more than me, Jack, it doesn't mean you get to tell me what I should and shouldn't want.'

'Sophia, do you have any idea of the effect you have over me?' He raked an unsteady hand through his hair, turned away from her and came back, then reached for her and stopped. 'I want to kiss you so badly right now, and I don't care who sees!'

It wasn't what she'd expected. It wasn't anything close, and before she could really think about it she was reaching out for his jumper and grabbing a fistful as she pulled him into the outer hallway. Noah's present was crushed between them as she pressed her lips to his. Hungrily, she moved over him, *her* mouth driving it, *her* tongue. There was nothing soft or sweet about her now. She wanted him to know she was all woman and she knew her own mind and would take what she wanted.

As soon as his hands lifted to her hair, his lips softening beneath her own, she pulled back and stared him down. 'Just because this is new to me, Jack, it doesn't mean I'm not a quick learner and it *doesn't* make me weak.'

And then she left him, his clothing still ruffled, his hair too as he sucked in air and she walked into the flat to join the lively party ahead. She took a moment to pat down her appearance, to wipe her lips and catch her breath. Samantha would likely think she'd applied an extra layer of blusher, not kissed the face off Lily's egotistical and far too appealing father.

As for the apology she owed him, that would have to wait until later. If he dared to be alone with her again.

What had she done?

'Sphea! At last!' Lily ran up to her, her face aglow, her happiness adding to the endorphin rush already in her system and she grinned wide.

'Hey, kiddo, you having a good time?'

'The best.' She nodded fiercely, her arms wrapped around her legs.

'I'm glad.'

'Yes, where've you been, Auntie Sophia?' Sam's tone was loaded. 'It's lucky Jack hung around else it would be utter carnage—I'm talking swinging from the chandelier stuff.'

Sophia laughed. 'You don't even have a chandelier.'

'Yes, well, at least you're here now. Drink?'

'Please.'

Samantha disappeared off to get her one and she sought out the birthday boy amongst the kids huddled into the living area. 'Hey, Noah, I've got something for you here.'

She lifted the present up so he could see it and he bounded over. 'Thank you, Aunt Soph!'

'You're welcome,' she said, bending down as he gave her a hug and a kiss to the cheek. 'Happy birthday!'

He took the present and raced to the sofa, his friends and Lily all circling around him as he opened it. She looked back in the direction of the door, to where Jack still was. What was he doing?

'Here…' Sam appeared at her side, a glass of fizz in each hand and offered one out to her. 'Drink this; we're going to need it.'

Sophia laughed but gratefully accepted it, her eyes back on Noah as he ripped through the packaging but her head returned to Jack and his absence. She also knew Sam had noticed, the way her friend's eyes kept flicking to her, trying to read her, and any minute now she would ask, *What have you done with Jack?*

She threw back a gulp of fizz and pondered her

answer. *Sorry, hon, I think I just accosted him in the hallway and now he's run for his life.*

'You okay?' Sam eventually asked. 'You've looked strangely flushed since the moment you walked in.'

Sophia almost choked on the bubbles. *Trust Sam to say it how it is.*

'I'm fine.'

'You sure, 'cos you've only gotta say the word and I'll go sort him out.'

She gave Sam a warning glare that was half *Thank you* and half *Don't even think about it.* She just prayed Sam didn't come right out and say something to him.

Maybe she shouldn't have spilled her all to her friend last Sunday. But when Sam had turned up on her doorstep at the crack of dawn, a tasty bag of fresh pastries and two coffees in hand, with a please-let-me-live-vicariously-through-you look in her eye, Sophia hadn't been able to keep her mouth shut. And, to be fair, Sam had been a good listener, a good listener who'd sympathised greatly with the nature of her predicament, but also advised in no uncertain terms that Sophia should be in it for the fun and shouldn't expect more. She'd also been quick to add that should he hurt her she'd go after him with her—

'Nutcracker at the ready, Soph…'

She looked to the doorway and, sure enough, Jack had returned…

* * *

Jack leaned back against the wall and counted to ten, then twenty…then thirty because there was no way he was walking back into a kids' party in this…situation. He glanced down then breathed some more. His tent-like situation wasn't the worst of his problems either. It was the fact that he'd been so close to suggesting they end this the one way he knew how: in his bed.

And then what?

She'd have given him her virginity and he would fly away to his next destination—in this case Tokyo—like it meant nothing.

No, just no.

Then why was he still so torn?

Because you want her and you know she's different; you just don't understand why.

And it was his job to understand everything: the people he did business with, the people he employed, his daughter. But Sophia was an enigma—the power she wielded over him, the all-consuming need she sparked.

Maybe he really had been off the dating scene too long. He'd had plenty of offers over the years, but none had tempted him. Not like this. And again, there was the problem—it was her. He wanted her and no one else would do.

Was he really worried about her and her innocence, or was it his own ability to move on that he doubted?

He shook off the crazed thought and headed back inside. Sex could be just that. Sex. It didn't need to be complicated with more so long as they were honest from the outset.

He would let Lily have her fun, enjoy time with her peers and when it was all over he would take this up with Sophia. They would thrash it out until they both understood what the other wanted from this and there'd be no overstepping that agreement.

He couldn't deny that the prospect excited him far too much to let his worry back in. There would be time for worry later, much later, when he was far away from London and the past.

'Ah, Jack, thought you'd got lost between here and the front door for a second,' Samantha teased, turning away and picking up a chilled bottle of beer. 'Here's one I prepped for you.'

She walked up to him, her eyes seeing far too much, he was sure. What exactly did she know? Had Sophia talked to her? And what was she thinking now as she narrowed her gaze on him? Why did women *have* to talk?

'Cheers!' she said, offering up her drink.

'Cheers.'

He chinked the bottle against her glass and took a long pull of the cold liquid, realising not only how much he needed its cooling temperature but that he hadn't drunk straight from the bottle in a long time.

He heard a giggle behind Samantha, an easily recognisable giggle, and he looked over her head to see Sophia's sparkling blue eyes on him.

He raised his brow at her. 'What?'

'Nothing…just the sight of you slumming it with the rest of us, no champagne in sight… It tickles me.'

His eyes didn't leave Sophia's laughing ones; the urge to kiss her was overwhelming. 'So, it tickles you, does it?'

He stepped around Samantha and headed towards her.

Her eyes flared, her smile turning wary. 'Uh-huh.'

'If you want something real to tickle you, I'm game.'

She backed up. 'You wouldn't dare?'

'Wouldn't I?'

She backed up some more, finding her thighs meeting the side table that sported plastic cups, juice jugs and a birthday cake.

'You've nowhere to run, princess.'

She was laughing and serious at once, the conflicting dance making her all the more appealing, all the more flushed. 'Lily! Lily! Come and rescue me. Your daddy's going to tickle me.'

'Coming, Sphea!' came his daughter's battle cry, followed by an all-male cry from the rest of the mini-partygoers and suddenly he was attacked, legs, arms, neck, the kids doing their best to take him down. He laughed, swinging this way and that as the kids giggled and cheered each other on.

Sophia relaxed as she realised she was safe, her hand reaching out for his beer bottle as he passed it to her shortly before hitting the floor. And then he became a crawling tickle monster, being tickled and tickling back with more children than he could count.

'Go easy on him, kids,' Samantha cooed. 'We don't want to scare Lily's daddy away altogether.'

Sophia laughed, her genuine amusement lifting him inside and making all manner of bruising from the over-zealous tickling he was taking worth it.

She definitely wasn't scared or fearful of him, of whatever this was, now. Her behaviour, even her words on the doorstep, told him that. And if she wasn't scared, then why should he be?

They were grown adults going into this with their eyes wide open… What could possibly go wrong?

CHAPTER NINE

'THANKS SO MUCH for sticking around to help me clean up, guys.' Samantha pulled Sophia into a hug. 'Dan will be home just in time to enjoy the magic of the delayed sugar rush.'

'And two extra kids too. You're brave to add a sleepover to the mix!' Sophia laughed, pulling back to look her friend in the eye. 'You're such a good mum.'

'Or crazy,' she joked. 'I'm not sure which.'

Samantha turned to Jack and pulled him into a hug too, surprising him with the gesture if the wide-eyed look over her friend's shoulder was anything to go by.

'Thank you, Jack. It's not often the dads stick around; you're a bona fide modern father.' She patted him on the chest as she released him. 'I'm *très* impressed.'

Sophia forced back the mental retort that he'd only done it because he didn't trust either of them to take care of his daughter. It was bitter and, in truth, though it might have factored in his decision to stay, he'd clearly had fun. More importantly, so had the kids. And he'd been a fully fledged part of that fun. He hadn't stood in the shadows keeping watch; he'd got involved and been a huge hit with all of Noah's friends. A huge hit with Sam too.

As for Sophia, well, she already knew there was no hope for her...

'It was a novel experience.' He rubbed the back of his neck. His smile was...*bashful*. And making him all the more appealing with it. 'Enjoy the sleepover.'

'I will. I have wine and I'm leaving Dan in charge!'

They all laughed, save for Lily, who tugged on her daddy's hand. 'I wish I could sleep over.'

Samantha scooted down to give her a squeeze. 'With *three stinky boys*, you really don't, but you never know, maybe we can sort something for another time. I'd be glad of the female company.' She looked up at Jack with a smile. 'She's always welcome.'

'Yes, well...' He cleared his throat and placed his hand on Lily's shoulder. 'I think you're right, tonight's not the night for it.'

'But some other time, Daddy?'

'We'll see.'

'That means no.'

Sophia took pity on him and said, 'I might have an alternative idea.'

Lily looked at her, all hopeful.

'If your daddy agrees, you could sleep at mine?'

Lily beamed, her hopeful gaze now set on her father.

There was a crash from inside the flat and Samantha winced. 'Right, on that note, I'm leaving you guys to it. I just hope that noise has nothing to do with Dan's latest construction model!'

She dashed inside and closed the door, leaving Sophia and Lily looking up at a shell-shocked Jack. 'Well… I…what, tonight?'

'Sure.' She shrugged. 'I have no plans, the guest room is made up, and we can watch the latest Disney film and eat ice cream, just like any good sleepover. Maybe I could even paint your nails?'

Lily let out an excited squeal and started bobbing up and down. 'Please, Daddy, please, pretty please, pretty, pretty please.'

Sophia was pushing him. Deep down she knew it. She was toying with his trust boundaries and almost willing him to fail. Because if he failed, it would make it so much easier to keep some distance between them. To let him go in a week's time and not wonder what if.

'Daddy…' Lily tugged on his hand some more. 'Please, I've never had a sleepover.'

'I'm just not sure how it would work.'

'It's really simple.' Sophia smiled up at him. 'Lily and I get the quilt off the bed, plonk ourselves in front of the TV and eat copious amounts of ice cream, pausing only to paint our nails.'

'And me?'

Her smile became a confused frown. 'You?'

'Where would I fit into this sleepover?'

'You'd like a manicure too?' Her voice was elevated, her panic obvious.

'Oh, yes, that would be fun!' Lily blurted, nothing amiss in her world. 'I could paint yours, Daddy, you could do Sphea's, and Sphea could do mine.'

Sophia spluttered, unable to keep the weird choking sound in. This was *not* what she had in mind. But it clearly worked for Jack, whose face had lit up dramatically.

'Something wrong, Sophia?'

'No,' she hurried out.

'So, can we, Daddy?'

'If Sophia is happy, then I'm all for it.'

'But…but I only have the one spare room. You'd have to share or take the sofa.'

'The sofa is good enough for me.'

'Right… Okay then, sleepover it is.' She turned in a dazed fashion and headed to her apartment across the hall, hearing Lily's laugh following her.

'Isn't it funny how Noah has two friends staying over and now Sphea has two as well, Daddy?'

'Yes.' Jack chuckled. 'Very.'

She could feel his eyes burning into her back and caught the husky edge to his voice. *Funny* was not the word she would have used.

Dangerous. Yes.

Funny. *No.*

When I say I want you I mean it…

She'd really said that. Really, really said that. Against this very wall, just a few hours ago… promising him so much and now…now he was about to have a sleepover, at her place, with his *daughter…* No, no, *no!*

Clever move, Sophia Lambert. Clever and stupid and so messed-up.

She'd wanted him to trust her with Lily. She'd wanted him to feel comfortable leaving his daughter with her, just her. Not only for Lily's sake so she wasn't missing out, but because, though he might not trust Sam, he *should* trust her.

And instead she'd ended up with both. Daddy and daughter. In her apartment. For a night!

What exactly was the etiquette for a sleepover when the child came with their father and you wanted that man so badly you propositioned him outside a kids' party?

She had no idea, but she'd better work it out sharpish…and make sure he knew whatever it was too.

Jack stood back as Sophia slotted the key in the lock. Somewhere at the back of his mind there was an almighty reel of panicked nonsense telling him this was a bad idea. But right now his daughter was happy and he…well, he was curious.

He wasn't even sure that was the right word,

but when Sophia had had him pinned to the wall and taken what she wanted with the promise of—

He quit the recollection as she turned to look at him. Here it came, the excuse, the get-out clause. He could sense it in the nervous flicker of her lashes, her sweetly parted lips that she dampened and ran her teeth over…

'Did you—?' She broke off, colour streaking high across her cheekbones. 'Did you want to go back to the hotel and get some things?'

Things? He frowned, then stood to attention just as quickly. *She means clothes, you idiot!*

Her brow lifted. 'Like clothes…toiletries…' her eyes flicked to Lily '… Baby Bear?'

Lily gasped. 'Baby Bear! I *need* Baby Bear.'

'No problem. I'll call Ms Archer, ask her to pack a bag and get it couriered across.'

'Of course. Couriered over…right.'

'If you'd rather we arranged it for another night…?'

'But, Daddy, we leave in seven sleeps. When will we have time?'

'Seven sleeps?' Sophia repeated, her hand still resting over the keys in the lock. He wanted to deny it, to say he had longer, that they had no intention of leaving yet, but that would be a lie and served no purpose other than to make her, and thus him, feel better. It wouldn't change the inevitable. The takeover deal was almost done and dusted; they had no reason to stay. None at all.

'Yes, we fly Saturday afternoon.'

She lowered her lashes and took a small breath. 'Then tonight it is.'

She pushed open the door and flicked on the lights, the soft white walls giving off a warm ambience as opposed to the grey Samantha had opted for next door. Lily raced in behind her and started poking her head through the open doors.

'It's just like Noah's!'

'Yes.' Sophia smiled at her, then turned to Jack, her lips softening a little and doing something weird to his chest.

'Are you sure—?'

'Where am I sleeping, Sphea?' Lily bustled up to them, interrupting his impulsive need to check she was truly all right with this.

'Come on, I'll show you.' Sophia offered out her hand and Lily grinned at her, her obvious affection for this woman who'd only been in their lives a week chiming with his own. 'While Daddy makes his important call to Ms Archer…'

'Yes, right, I'll get on with it.' His voice sounded gruff, his chest too full to breathe properly. He smiled to hide it, but he wasn't so sure he'd succeeded, not if the questioning look Sophia sent over Lily's head was anything to go by.

'Okay?' she mouthed.

He nodded quickly and turned away, pulling his mobile from his jacket and dialling Ms Archer. Ever efficient, she answered promptly and he was done in five. It took him another five to compose himself enough to join the two women who had put him in this alien position. Their chatter was incessant and he only had to follow it to find them in the open-plan kitchen-cum-diner-cum-living area.

Sophia was warming something on the hob while Lily sat on a stool at the breakfast bar which separated the kitchen from the rest of the space.

'I've had one request for a fully loaded hot chocolate,' she said, looking at him over her shoulder. 'What can I get you?'

He slipped onto the barstool next to his daughter. 'What's a fully loaded hot chocolate?'

'It's topped with marshmallows and cream, Daddy.'

'Sounds good.'

'You fancy one too?'

He could hear the surprise in Sophia's voice and laughed. 'Why not?'

She shook her head. 'You're full of surprises, Jack McGregor.'

'What? Can't a grown man indulge once in a while?'

That high colour was back in her face and this time he knew it was the thoughts at play in her head, thoughts that he'd triggered by the double meaning of *indulge*. She gave him a small smile and went back to stirring the milk in the pan. Next to him Lily was sifting through what looked to be mail.

'Hey, don't be so nosy, kiddo.'

'I'm just looking.'

'That's precisely my point.'

'It's okay,' Sophia said. 'It's just the junk mail I didn't have time to go through at work. It's mainly brochures and stuff. Sometimes there's some interesting—'

'Wow! Look at this, Daddy!' Lily had a brochure spread out before her, her eyes like saucers as she pointed one of her small fingers at what looked like a giant bubble. 'You can stay in one of these and look at the stars *all* night!'

He grinned. 'Looks like fancy camping to me.'

'But look at the sky, Daddy. Does it really look like that or have they just done something with a computer to make it all…fancy?'

'That's the lights of aurora.'

'Aurora?'

'Aurora borealis, the northern lights.'

'Bore what? It looks like magic.' She lifted the brochure and turned it this way and that, her eyes wide, fascinated. 'Magic in the sky.'

'It's amazing, isn't it?' Sophia said to her as she pulled mugs out of a cupboard and scooped chocolate powder into each.

'Have you ever been?' Lily asked.

'No.' She stirred the milk into the cups. 'I'm not good with snow and to see it at its best you need to go in winter.'

'I love snow!'

Sophia gave a soft laugh. 'Most kids do.'

Her voice had turned distant, her eyes on the task in hand but unseeing. Was she thinking of her sister? The memory of that tale sent a shiver running through him now and the impulse to reach out for her was overpowering.

'Can I help?' he asked, coming up behind her, his hand gentle on her lower back.

She gave him a smile that didn't quite reach her eyes and his chest ached for her, his own smile filled with understanding, compassion.

'It's okay; I'm almost done.' She went back to the hot chocolate, squirting in cream and sprinkling on marshmallows with a dramatic flourish designed to hide it all. *'Voila!'*

She lifted two of the mugs and carried them to the counter, while he scooped up the third.

'These are impressive.'

She quirked a brow at him. 'You can say it.'

'Say what?'

'They're a cardiac arrest in a cup.'

'A cardy what?' Lily said, her brow wrinkling as she reached out for the one nearest to her and her eyes became fishbowls once more.

Sophia grimaced at Jack as she mouthed a *sorry* and he just smiled at her. 'Don't worry, I don't think even that would put her off.'

She blushed. 'Can't have a hot choc without all the trimmings. It's criminal.'

Lily laughed. 'Now I get it—cardy arrest. You are funny, Sphea.'

He laughed and shook his head. 'Isn't she just?'

Sophia looked to him, her own laughter sparkling in her eyes. He lifted the mug to his lips, felt the cream tickle at his nose and saw her eyes lower to the sight, her blush deepening. What wouldn't he give to know what she was thinking? 'You want to explain how you drink it?'

'I quite like watching you work it out.'

He cleaned off the tip of his nose and watched as she closed her mouth over a marshmallow and some cream and felt his body tighten. His hand clenched tight around his mug.

'Mmm, it's so good,' Sophia murmured. 'How's yours, Lily?'

'Perfect,' his daughter said, sticking her finger straight in and scooping up the topping, then popping it into her mouth with zero elegance. Mood officially killed. 'Dee-licious! Isn't it, Daddy?'

'Yup.' Not that he had tasted yet...

They all moved to the small dining table and Lily dragged the brochure into the middle of them, the double-page spread open with the bubble-like hotel room surrounded by woodland and the aurora lights flooding the sky. There were images all the way around it showing the various sights Iceland had to offer: waterfalls, the black sand beach, the basalt stacks, geo-thermal pools, geysers… It really was a sight and his daughter was clearly fascinated.

'It's such a great concept,' Sophia said, spying his focus. 'Being able to sleep under the stars, all warm and cosy with a three-hundred-and-sixty-degree view of it all.'

And yet she wouldn't go because of the white stuff also liberally sprinkled throughout the shot. He leaned closer to her, his arm brushing against hers. 'It is incredible.'

'But is it real or have they just made it up?'

'What, the bubbles or the sky?'

'It's all real,' Sophia said, her finger swirling over the bubble in the picture. 'This is in Iceland.'

'Iceland? Have I ever been to Iceland, Daddy?'

'No, neither of us have.'

'I'd like to go some time.'

'I'm sure you would.'

'Could we all go?'

Sophia choked on her chocolate and turned away.

Jack decided that there was no way to answer his daughter's impulsive question so instead he asked her another. 'What was your favourite bit about today?'

Lily pressed her lips together, looked to the ceiling and hummed. 'All of it! Having friends to play with—Noah has so many friends—and then when we all jumped on you and that was so funny.'

'Funny for you maybe…' he rolled his shoulders '…my body isn't so sure.'

Lily laughed, giving him a playful shove. 'You were great, Daddy. I'm lucky to have a daddy like you.'

His chest swelled, even his eyes pricked, and then he caught the warmth in Sophia's gaze and he was hooked.

'But we have a problem…'

He dragged his eyes to Lily, surprised by her sudden downturn, even more so by her solemn frown.

Uh-oh.

'How do I get friends for my birthday party in Tokyo?'

CHAPTER TEN

'A SLEEPOVER AT the age of thirty—who would have thought it?'

Jack's voice was low as he tried not to disturb a snoozing Lily who was lying between them, propped up on pillows with the blanket covering them all.

'I still can't believe she roped us into getting the sofa bed out just to watch the film.' Sophia didn't look at him as she said it; her eyes were fixed on the TV screen and not on the proximity of his. It was too snug, too easy, lying like this with the lights down low, the TV playing a movie she could remember nothing of, and all in her own domain.

It was easy to forget who Jack was. From the moment he'd got on all fours at the party and rolled around with the kids, taken a slop of cream to the nose with his unmanly drink and cosied up on her ancient sofa with her well-worn tartan blanket, she had lost sight of what was real. Because she didn't just want him, she realised; she wanted so much more.

'I think I was too busy worrying about her up-coming birthday I'd have agreed to anything.'

Now she looked at him and saw the lines of concern creasing his face as the colours of the TV danced over them. 'You're really worried about it?'

'It's not just today. I've been thinking a lot about what you've said, about her having no base and being unable to set down roots or make real friends of her own.'

'I'm sorry.' She felt guilty even though she knew she'd been right to raise it. 'But I think it's important for her to have all that, although I know it makes things difficult for you.'

'Perhaps.'

'Have you thought more about speaking to her grandmother?'

He sent her a quick look and sighed. 'Yes. I have. And I will. It won't be easy, but I think it's worth a shot.'

'From what you've said she'll likely have aunts and uncles close to her own age, family that she can play with, grow up with.'

'That would mean coming back to the UK.'

'And you're not ready for that?'

He worked his shoulders into the pillow behind him, under the pretence of getting comfortable, but she had the feeling it was more to mask the pain of what that thought brought.

'It's not going to be a quick fix though; it's not

going to help with the imminent arrival of her birthday.'

'No, I guess not. Do you have to go to Tokyo? Perhaps you could stay longer…' She couldn't stop the spark of hope, the idea of having them around longer too appealing to ignore.

'You could borrow Noah and his friends?' She gave a teasing smile. 'They'd love to see you again, I'm sure.'

He laughed, the sound sending a shiver of delight through her. 'It's an idea… I just wish things were different.'

He went quiet, his eyes distant, and she reached over to place a reassuring hand on his above the blanket. 'It seems to me that you're on the right track though. This time next year things *could* be very different for her.'

He gave her a small smile. 'Thank you.'

'For what?'

'For making me see sense.'

She laughed softly. 'I didn't do anything.'

Their eyes caught and she felt that connection between them sizzle to life. 'You've done more than you could possibly know.'

Her lips parted as she tried to take in air, to cope with the warmth spreading through her body. 'I'm glad I could help.'

'Me too.' He looked to Lily between them. 'I'd best get her to bed.'

She nodded, removing her hand to look down

at his sleeping daughter, who had the brochure of Iceland open and pressed into her chest. 'She's beautiful.'

'You both are.'

'Jack...' She shook her head, half brushing off his remark, half treasuring it as she picked the brochure up and climbed off the bed.

'Just speaking the truth.'

She couldn't stop the smile that touched her lips or the way his words turned her insides to a soft, gooey mess as she took the brochure and the empties into the kitchen and placed them on the counter. It felt so surreal having them here... and at the same time so right. She'd never thought herself lonely before, but when they left she just knew it would be different.

She lifted the brochure Lily had loved so much and flicked it open to the double-page spread, placing it down on the counter and tracing her fingers over the see-through dome, the bed with the family of three sitting upon it gazing up at Aurora and the stars.

'She's out for the count,' Jack said, walking back into the room. 'Didn't even murmur when I tucked her in.'

Sophia didn't look up. She was too lost in the image beneath her fingers and the idea that was forming.

'I know what you can do for her birthday,' she rushed out in whispered excitement. 'And she'll love every second. And you won't need an instant family or instant friends to do it.'

She sensed him frown. 'What?'

She slid the brochure across the counter to him and tapped a finger on the picture of the dome. 'This!'

He laughed. 'It's a great idea, but surely it'll be fully booked by now.'

'The resort is new. I only have the brochure because I'm in the industry. They're running some special launch stays prior to their grand opening. I could put in a call, see what there is?'

'I don't know...'

'You saw how much she loved it and you know how much she loves the stars. Even if you don't see the northern lights, she'd be in her element with the snow, the waterfalls, the amazing scenery... She'd love it all.'

He ran a hand through his hair as he looked down at the brochure and then grinned. 'You're right, of course you are.'

'I'm always right,' she teased, looking up into his eyes and realising how much closer she'd stepped as she'd worked on convincing him.

'Is that so?' He turned into her, his hands reaching for her waist, and she had no desire to pull away. This was what she wanted. What she needed.

She leaned into him, her 'Yes...' a whisper, a plea, as he bowed his head and she tilted her own back. His lips brushed over her own, her sharp inhale a striking contrast to the softness of his mouth and its coaxing pressure.

'Sophia…' He parted her lips with his tongue, brushing against hers with teasing intent. As if he was savouring her, exploring her, drawing her out, the inner desire that she'd never known existed until now, until him.

She raised her fingers to his chest and felt his warmth, the hard muscle beneath his jumper, and travelled higher still until her hands were in his hair, holding him to her as he took the same journey over her body.

She was aching, an incessant, thudding pang spreading through her lower belly that promised so much pleasure.

He broke from her mouth to travel along her jawline, his stubble teasing the same path, his tongue, his teeth—*oh, yes.* She clung to his head, her own arching back as he brushed against her ear, his lips teasing with his words. 'Never have I wanted someone like I want you.'

'Take me then, Jack, please,' she sighed against him, her breasts pressing into his chest, her leg hooking around him to draw him closer, to hold him near. 'I need you.'

And he needed her too. She could feel his hardness pressing urgently against her, could feel his desire rising with her own, his breath as short. He came back to her mouth, this time hungry, his tongue plundering, and she was ready, willing, waiting. She gave it back to him in return, leaving him in no doubt as to how much she wanted this.

He grabbed her by the hips and lifted her onto the counter, wrapped her legs around himself as he came back to claim her lips.

'This is crazy,' he rasped against her. 'Crazy and out of control.'

'Crazy but so good.' She pulled his lips back to hers, her hands dropping to the hem of his jumper as she tugged it over his head and leaned back. She had to see him. She needed to. His dark skin glowed in the light of her kitchen, the sheen of perspiration reflecting in the light, his short breaths rippling his pecs. 'You're beautiful.'

He gave a gentle scoff. 'I'm a man.'

'So?' She looked up into his blazing greys, so dilated with desire, and the next words came out gruff with her own need. 'You're still beautiful.'

And then she was kissing him again, feeling his hot hands on her bare skin as they slipped beneath her jumper, her nerve-endings coming alive, savouring every sweep of his hands, every light brush of his fingers as they smoothed beneath the band of her bra. She was losing her mind—it was the only way to describe the intense rush of feeling inside her.

'I want you, Sophia.' He yanked the jumper over her head, her hair tumbling around her bare shoulders as he threw her jumper to the side.

'I want you too.'

He lifted her from the counter and walked her to the sofa bed, easing her down before stretching out beside her, his mouth hot against her lips, her neck. Her hands raked down his back as he travelled over her skin, making her writhe and plead. 'Please, Jack, please.'

She wanted to say more, so much more. She wanted to say, *Be my first*, wanted him to know what that meant to her, but he already knew. Just as she knew the reminder would stop him, as it had before, and so she clamped down on her bottom lip and told him with her body what she wanted.

'Come with us, Sophia—come with us to Iceland.'

Her eyes shot open and she gazed down at him, hardly daring to believe the question and knowing at the same time that she couldn't. The thought, the idea of being surrounded by her fear, by the past, by the snow… She shook her head and shifted beneath him to remind him of her body, of what she wanted in that moment. What he so wanted too.

'You can't ask me that, Jack. Don't ask me that.'

He raised himself up over her, his elbows planted either side of her body to bear his weight. 'Why not?'

'Because I can't. *We* can't.'

He kissed her until she was breathless, panting. 'Why?'

'We don't even know they'll be available for her birthday yet.'

'That doesn't matter. They will be available at some point and I want you to come.'

She shook her head, the emotions clawing at her throat and her chest, making it hard to breathe. 'We both know this has to end and that the longer we spend together with Lily, the more likely it is that she will become attached too.'

His eyes were so serious now as they blazed into hers. The 'too' spoke volumes; it told him that fear protected her own heart, but did it protect his, as well?

'That's not the whole truth, is it?' he pressed, probing for more, probing for her to admit that she feared being faced with her past. All it took was one harmless-looking snowflake, the ice forming over her windshield, and the shivers would start.

'It's enough.'

He shook his head, one hand stroking her cheek and catching a tear she hadn't known was there. 'You need to stop living in fear of your past, Sophia.'

He kissed her to soften his words and she clamped her eyes shut over the rising swell of emotion within. 'You've taught me that; you've made me realise that avoiding a base, avoiding

London, is running from it. And by doing it, Lily has suffered.'

She kept her eyes closed as the tears refused to stop. He was right. She'd been a hypocrite to tell him the same and not realise it was exactly how she'd been behaving all along.

'Come with us. Not because I ask you, not because it would make Lily happy to have you there… Come because you want to. Come because you are ready to move on from it.'

She nodded, her eyes still clamped shut.

'Look at me, Sophia.'

Slowly she did as he asked, her hands coming up to gently stroke his back. 'Come because you want to be with us.'

She wet her lips as she stared up into his eyes. She saw so much—so much that she could almost believe, almost convince herself that it wasn't just her falling hard and fast. It was him too. And that was what had her kissing him so hard that she could barely breathe and he reciprocated, his arms slipping around her as he rolled her on top of him.

He pressed her away just long enough to ask, 'Is that a yes?'

'Yes, Jack, it's a yes.'

He didn't know what to think, didn't know how to be rational about this, to talk himself down from what he was about to do. The truth was he wasn't capable of clear thought. He wanted her more than he had ever wanted anyone, and it felt so right, so natural, so impossible to resist.

He rolled her back underneath him and kissed her, the emotion taking hold of his heart and driving every move he made. He was caught up in her, in what she brought to both him and Lily. And he wanted more. More sense of family, of belonging. He could feel the shift underway inside him, the beginnings of hope for a future, the possibility that maybe he could love her as she deserved and accept such love in return.

That was why he'd pleaded with her to come to Iceland. He knew the magnitude of what it meant for her personally to face her fear, and he knew he wanted to be right by her side when she took that leap.

He didn't know what the future held, but he knew that this was what they both wanted.

He deepened his kiss, one hand smoothing down her front to find the button of her jeans as his other stroked through her hair. He stripped her layer by layer, himself too, with the sense that it wasn't just their bodies being exposed but their hearts too.

You do this and you can't go back. You do this and you're promising more.

He bowed his head, his eyes shut tightly against her naked beauty. 'Sophia…'

He dragged in air, fighting for control over his desire. She answered him with her hands in his hair pulling him to her lips, her bare legs wrapping around his lower body, urging him closer. 'Please, Jack.'

He could hear the lust thickening her voice, the lust and so much more…

'Jack?'

He lifted his head, opened his eyes to see hers glistening back at him in the low light of the TV and his heart pulsed in his chest.

'Are you sure? There can be no going back, no…'

She released his hair, smoothing her palms around to his cheeks. 'Yes, Jack, I want it to be you.'

His breath rasped out of him, a bittersweet happiness choking up his throat. He moved away to seek out his jeans, his wallet, and the protection he had there. He took it out, sheathing himself, all the while feeling her eyes on him, the strength of her need, the sense that this was right, that this was what they both wanted keeping him moving.

He came back to her, their gazes locked together, a thousand words passing between them as he moved slowly, merging their bodies, surrounding himself in her. He wanted to say so much, promise so much…but it was all he could do to control this, to keep it slow.

He felt her resistance, felt her stiffen beneath him and the tension locking her legs tightly around him. He stilled, sweeping his hand over her hair, his nose brushing against hers as he whispered, 'I don't want to hurt you.'

Her eyes glistened further as she shook her head, her legs drawing him in. 'You won't, Jack. You're not.'

She kissed him—kissed him until he could think of nothing but claiming her heart as she had his, forcing out the guilt that tried to break in anew.

You won't hurt her... You won't hurt her... You won't...

Sophia clutched her glass of water to her chest and stared at the kitchen clock. Three a.m. glared back at her. *Three a.m.* and there was a gorgeous naked man asleep in her sofa bed and she was sitting at her breakfast bar, freshly showered with her PJs on and wishing she could climb straight back in with him.

Hence why she was looking at the clock and not at him. Because the temptation was too great and the risk that she would fall asleep again, only to have Lily wander in and find them, was too high.

It was bad enough she'd fallen asleep the first time, bad enough that they both had, but it had been blissful in the aftermath and she had been too content to move. As had he apparently.

And when she'd woken up to Jack's arm locked around her middle and the initial shock of being in bed with a man had passed, she'd found herself cocooned in his body warmth, soothed by his gentle snore, his scent, and she hadn't wanted to move. She'd let the night play back to her, along with the soreness of what they had shared, and her whole body had flushed with reignited heat and a strange bashfulness.

She'd been torn between staying and showering, and in the end it had been the thought that Lily could wake up that had spurred her into moving. It was one thing for Jack to wake and see her in that tangled mess, but not Lily. She wasn't sure where this turn in their relationship had left them, but she knew it wasn't in a solid enough place for Lily to learn of it.

Tomorrow—*no, later today*—they could talk. They could agree how they should be for Lily's sake and—

'Elena!'

She almost dropped her glass as he cried out. She looked back to the bed, to where he writhed and rolled, his arm flinging out, his face creased up in pain as his chest heaved.

She put the glass down and shot across the room, reaching out for him as she lowered herself to the bed. It didn't matter that it was another woman he called for, another woman who haunted his dreams; she was the one who could be there for him.

She cradled his head against her hip and gently shushed him, her fingers stroking through his hair, thankful that his features started to relax and his breathing settled.

She looked up to the hallway, to where her bedroom door lay, and knew it was useless now; she was his captive whether he intended her to be or not.

'Elena… Elena…' He writhed against her, his dead wife's name on his lips, and though she didn't want it to, her heart ached anyway. Was this how it was for him every night, Elena haunting his dreams? Or had what they'd shared triggered it?

And if it was the latter, what did it mean for them?

If she were to believe what he had told her, he'd never loved Elena, not in the way he felt she deserved. But he'd also said he could never feel for Sophia what he felt *she* deserved.

She thought about all he had said to her, about his request that she join him and Lily in Iceland, that she face her fears with him by her side. Surely that had to mean he felt more? Wasn't that why she'd wanted him to make love to her, why she'd wanted him to be her first, because regardless of what he felt for her, she knew she already felt so much more for him?

Her fingers stilled over his hair, her eyes intent on the sight of him lying beside her.

*Felt so much more…*she really did…it was too late to stop it, to hit rewind.

And even as she accepted it as fact, she knew she couldn't tell him, not yet. He wasn't ready to hear it. He would sooner run the other way than accept that another woman cared for him.

She wasn't scared of Iceland, the snow, the past. She was scared of the future and the knowledge that what she wanted above all else was a life with him and Lily.

Jack woke with a start to the smell of bacon cooking and his daughter's excited giggle.

'Do it again, Sphea, again!'

'Shh, you'll wake your daddy!' Sophia laughed as she said it, turning to smile down at Lily before lifting her gaze to him and freezing mid-movement, a frying pan outstretched before her. One second, two, and then her eyes softened into his, her smile lifting anew. 'Too late, he's up.'

'Daddy!' Lily raced across the room and he just had time to lock the blanket around his hips before she launched herself into his arms. 'Sphea's flipping pancakes!'

'She is?' He grinned at Sophia over his daughter's shoulder and saw her cheeks flush pink, like they so often did. He felt his heart blooming to life, the extent of what he felt for her hitting him full force. He waited for the panic, the worry… but there was none.

'I am.' She swept her forearm over her head to brush away the loose strands that fell around her face and turned back to place the pan on the heat. 'Can't have a Sunday morning without pancakes and bacon.' She glanced at him over her shoulder. 'Hungry?'

'Ravenous.' And he was, for so much more than food and, judging by the way her brows lifted, the way she ran her teeth over her bottom lip, she knew and felt it too.

Lily wriggled in his hold. 'Are you naked, Daddy? Didn't Ms Archer pack your pyjamas too?'

The innocent question had a foreign surge of heat spreading over his own cheeks… *Oh, dear.* 'I was very hot last night.'

He heard Sophia choke down a laugh and he tickled his daughter, her own laugh masking the telling one from the kitchen. 'Now, why don't you finish helping Sophia, while I freshen up and chuck on some clothes?'

'Okay,' she said on a ripple of laughter, her hair bouncing as she raced back into the kitchen.

'There are fresh towels in the bathroom,' Sophia said to him, her voice softly luring him over. He wanted to go to her, to place his hands on her hips and draw her into a morning kiss, one that was sure to rouse his body far too much and also give Lily the wrong impression.

Wrong impression?

What was the right one? What should he tell Lily about them? It was one thing to be spending this time together now, but how would it look when Sophia came to Iceland with them? How did he want it to look?

He showered quickly, throwing on some fresh clothes and returning to the comforting sounds and smells of the kitchen.

'You're just in time, Daddy! Look I've made a face...' She pushed her plate at him. Sure enough, there were two maple syrup blobs and a strip of bacon for a smile.

'Impressive.'

'Here's yours,' Sophia said, sliding a plate towards him, her skin delightfully pink from cooking, the brush of flour across her cheek teasing him. He reached out and brushed it away with his thumb, catching the way her breath hitched, her lips parted, and had to fight another urge to kiss her.

'You had a little flour...'

She traced the path of his fingers with her own, his need mirrored back at him. 'Thank you.'

'No, thank you.'

'Do I have any flour, Daddy?'

He lowered his gaze to his daughter and laughed; her timing was impeccable. 'You're covered.'

He rubbed both her cheeks with gusto as she wrinkled her nose and made a funny noise.

'All better,' he declared, planting a kiss on her

forehead and pulling up a stool before reaching for his plate. 'This looks amazing.'

'It won't beat the hotel breakfast,' Sophia said, 'but it'll certainly fill a hole. Coffee?'

'Please.'

She moved away and poured a freshly brewed pot into two awaiting mugs, returning with them both and offering one to him.

'Thank you,' he said, giving her a smile of gratitude that went so much further than breakfast. He had so much to be thankful for. So much that he couldn't put into words in front of Lily, not yet, but soon. Hopefully, very soon.

First, he needed to reach out to Elena's mum, to see if there truly was a chance for Lily to know her grandmother and her family.

Second, he needed to get Iceland booked and make his daughter's birthday one to remember.

And three, he needed to get his head around his feelings for Sophia, because now that he'd glimpsed how complete his life could be with her in it he didn't want to let it go. He wanted to make this work. He wanted to be worthy of her. He wanted to love her.

Which was lucky since he already did...

He shook his head at his own ramblings, his grin ridiculous, he was sure, but as he forked up a healthy chunk of pancake he realised he was actually too content to care.

CHAPTER ELEVEN

IT HAD BEEN over a week since Sophia had seen Jack and Lily, but it felt like so much longer.

They'd spent every evening together following that night, right up until their departure for Tokyo. Sophia would finish work and head up to the penthouse just in time for bath and bed, and sometimes Sophia would read, other times Jack, but it was always the three of them squeezed into the one bed with Lily and Baby Bear in the middle.

There'd been no more sleepovers though, much to Lily's disappointment. Work and it being a 'school night' were the excuses given but, in reality, Sophia knew they were trying to take things slow, to keep Lily from getting hurt, to hold themselves back too.

Everything was moving too fast, her own feelings for him—for Lily too—growing out of her control and with it came the fear. The fear of pushing him away, of confessing too much and having him run. The fear of the past, of his experience with Elena coming between them regardless of the seemingly comfortable happiness they had found.

Their 'us' was just too fragile.

And it wasn't just the fear of losing him; she would be losing Lily too, and the very idea had her tummy turning over and her feelings for him trapped deep inside, her lips sealed around them. Unless she was kissing him of course... She warmed even now with the thought, the remembered caress of his mouth over hers, the way he could coax her entire body to life with just the sweep of his lips, the stroke of his fingers...

'We're here, Ms Lambert.'

She jerked alert, a startled sound erupting from her throat as Jack's driver spoke into the silence. She met his eyes in the rear-view mirror, grateful he didn't look as if he'd noticed her teeny outburst or the crimson flush sure to exist in her cheeks now.

'Thank you.' She glanced out of the window and frowned. *Where's here?*

They weren't in the airport departures drop-off zone, that was certain; in fact, they were a good distance away from the terminal itself. She was about to query it when her door shifted open and she looked up to see Jack leaning in.

'Jack!' Her heart soared, the air leaving her lungs in a rush as she launched herself up, her arms wrapping around him.

A secret—yeah, right; her feelings were written in every movement she made.

'Hey,' he said against her ear, pressing a kiss there. 'It's good to see you.'

He breathed her in and then he lifted his head, forcing her back so he could scan her face. 'I missed you.'

'I missed you too,' she murmured, her eyes welling with her heart and she blinked the dampness away. 'Where are we?'

'My private hangar.'

'You're kidding.'

'Not at all.'

'No, of course you're not.' *What a stupid thing to say—this is Jack!*

'Sphea!' Lily came running up, wrapping her arms around them both and distracting Sophia from her self-deprecation. She crouched down and scooped her into a hug, the elation running through her obvious to anyone looking on. Her secret truly was no secret at all. 'I missed you.'

Lily squeezed her tightly. 'I missed you too.'

'Are you excited for your birthday trip?'

She nodded emphatically. 'Daddy has read your brochure with me every night.'

She looked up at Jack. 'Every night, hey?'

He chuckled. 'She can probably tell you more about where we're going than the people who live there.'

Sophia laughed as she stood back up. It was

then she saw the plane with its door open, staff and steps at the ready, the engine whirring through the brisk cold air. 'Is that…yours?'

There you go again with the naïve questions.

'It is.' Jack's grin turned lopsided. 'You ready to see inside?'

Was she? She felt nervous, out of place, suddenly uneasy. She turned away. 'I'll just get my things.'

'It's okay.' He took hold of her arm, bringing her back to him. 'My team will take care of your luggage.'

He offered out his hand and she tried for a smile, interlacing her fingers through his like she had come to do so often before they had left for Tokyo.

Lily took hold of her other hand and she smiled down at her.

'We're going to have so much fun,' the little girl cooed, her eyes bright and happy.

'That we are…' Sophia said softly, her eyes returning to the aircraft as they headed towards it together, the butterflies picking up inside her belly.

She knew she was silly to be surprised by it— the plane, the hangar—but she was. Surprised, awestruck, and deep down utterly unsettled. The opulence was a timely reminder of who Jack was and just how much she didn't belong in his world.

At least in her home, even in her place of work, she was able to forget all this and see him as Jack—*just* Jack. Not the billionaire business-man, the successful tycoon, the man in the press. And even though she feared her feelings for him, she had come to accept them. She'd even started to let in hope that he could feel the same, that there could be a future... At least it felt more realistic when they were away from all this.

I missed you...

Even now her lips lifted at his honest declara-tion from seconds before, one that she had quickly reciprocated and felt to her toes. His words teased her with that future again. But as she looked around her, taking in his private airfield, his staff, his private car that had delivered her, and back to his heaven-knew-how-expensive aeroplane, that acceptance of her feelings, that hope of a future took a hit.

Because this was the stuff of movies. Not real life.

And even Samantha had been cautious when Sophia had opened up to her about how she felt, about this trip and the possibility of there being more. She was her best friend and she actually *liked* Jack, but still she'd cautioned against getting in too deep, to keep her head out of the clouds and her feet grounded.

She gave a soft laugh as they paused before the

steps and Jack eyed her, his own smile cautious. 'Something funny?'

'Just something Samantha said. It's nothing important…' Nothing important but the exact opposite of what she was about to do as she started to follow Lily up into the plane.

There was no turning back now.

And in truth she didn't want to.

'Oh, my, Jack.' She couldn't keep the wonder out of her voice as she stepped inside the cabin and took in the plush interior, a mixture of creams and warm wood with inviting sofas, a large TV screen, a dining table, a kitchen one way and a bedroom at the other. It was as impressive as any hotel room and she couldn't believe where she was.

'You approve?' He slipped off his jacket and hooked it over the back of a leather recliner. He looked so at home, so at ease, and of course he would do; this was his domain. But Sophia…she really didn't know how to feel.

'It's incredible,' she said truthfully.

He smiled. 'Wait until you taste dinner.'

'Please tell me it's pizza, Daddy, and none of that fancy stuff we got last time.' Lily screwed up her face as she said it and he looked to Sophia with an apologetic grimace.

'I'm happy with pizza,' she said quickly, silently pleading, *Please let it be pizza*. Something normal, to help her feel normal.

'You are?'

'Absolutely.' He hesitated a second longer and then disappeared into the front of the plane as Lily clambered into one of the seats at the dining table and threw her bag on top of it.

'Come sit next to me, Sphea.' She patted the seat beside her and started pulling sheets of paper out of her bag. 'I want to show you my drawings.'

Sophia smiled and did as Lily asked, glancing down at the little sketches she started to spread out over the table.

'These are of us in Iceland!' she declared and, sure enough, the pictures were of the three of them doing various different things: sledging, having a snowball fight, building a snowman, lying inside a bubble looking up at the stars...

Sophia's smile grew, warmth spreading inside her chest and pushing out the unease, the uncertainty. What Lily dreamed of married so closely with what Sophia wanted too.

'Dinner crisis averted,' Jack said, rubbing his hands together as he returned to them, his own eyes falling to the pictures and making him pause. She watched his face, watched it flicker with some unguarded emotion and then the shutter fell, his eyes lifting to her. 'It means a slight delay to take-off, but we'll still be in Iceland for a decent time this evening.'

'Lovely.'

He looked back to Lily and gestured to all the sketches. 'You've been busy.'

Sophia could tell by his face he hadn't seen the pictures before and she had no idea how to gauge his reaction to them now.

'It helps when I can't sleep.'

'So that's why I keep finding your torch in bed with you?'

Lily gave him an impish grin. 'I like drawing.'

'And I *like* your drawings…' he slid into the seat beside Sophia, leaning forward to give his daughter a stern look '…but you still should have been sleeping.'

She gave a little huff and pulled out her fluffy pink pencil case, ready to create some more.

'I like them too,' Sophia said, ducking low to speak to her. 'Very much.'

And when she straightened again she felt his eyes on her, her own finding his just as swiftly.

'You do?' he asked softly.

'Yes.' And she knew then that they were both saying the same thing: that they liked it being the three of them, not just on paper but in real life, and hope sparked ever brighter inside.

'What shall I draw next, Sphea?'

She pulled her eyes from his and looked back to the pictures, her eyes settling on the sledging one, and for the briefest of seconds she felt the old familiar pang, the chill.

Jack reached out, his hand settling over hers to give it a gentle squeeze. 'You okay?'

She took a breath and gave him a small smile. She knew he'd picked up on the sudden wave of sadness and as she looked to his creased-up brow, his grey eyes soft with concern, she knew she was more than okay.

'Yes.' And with him by her side she would get through this trip and be all the stronger for it. 'I am.'

He returned her smile but he didn't release her hand, keeping it there as they both offered up ideas to Lily, who evaluated each and every one in the special way she had until she'd decided on a scene involving hot chocolate and a roaring fire.

They settled back like that, Lily drawing, Jack's hand on Sophia's, their chatter innocent enough for Lily's ears and so easy. They caught up on the past week, on what had happened with work, with Samantha and Noah. They ate pizza and played Snap with Lily. Everything was normal and relaxed. She could almost forget they were on a plane, if not for the occasional turbulence and the persistent hum of the engine.

Lily gave a huge yawn and scooted a little closer to Sophia's side.

'Tired, kiddo?'

She nodded and rested her head in Sophia's lap. She didn't ask, she didn't seek permission, she just did it and the move was so telling and touching.

'It's the middle of the night back in Tokyo,' Jack said softly, his eyes on his daughter in Sophia's lap. 'She's been going for hours now.'

'You both have,' she said, stroking Lily's hair.

'She's quite taken with you.'

She smiled. 'The feeling's mutual.'

'She's not the only one.' The sincerity of his voice, so close to her ear, had her entire body warming and her eyes returning to his. Was he saying…? Was he admitting…? She hoped so, so much.

He cleared his throat and looked back to Lily. 'The travelling has really taken its toll this time.'

'It is a lot in a short space of time. Have you thought more about settling somewhere more permanent?' She almost said *London* and realised it was too personal, too soon, and too close to what she wanted deep down for her own selfish reasons.

'I have and we will, soon. I'd like to spend a little time with Elena's family first, to see whether there is something worth saving there.'

'Have you spoken to her mother?'

His eyes turned distant. 'Yes.'

'And?'

His lips curved up a little. 'It was nice. *She* was nice. She also sounded beside herself that I'd called.'

'Beside herself in a good way?'

His eyes met with hers and she could see the lightness in them, the relief. 'In a very good way.

She wants to meet as soon as possible. She wanted to go all in—Lily, me, her husband and all three children, and though it was nice to hear her so excited, I'm not quite ready to expose Lily to that all at once.'

'Baby steps?'

'Yes, baby steps. I've decided to take Lily to meet her when we get back from Iceland. Then we can talk about meeting the rest of the family. I want to see how Lily takes to her first. I want her to drive this as much as me, if not more…'

Sophia smiled as she looked back to the girl fast asleep in her lap, her soft snore reaching up to them, her thick lashes, so like her father's, fanned out across her deep golden skin. Beautiful. Angelic. And Sophia felt her love for the little girl swell.

If she was to have Elena's family in her life then all the better, but Sophia wanted to be in that life too. She wanted to be in both of their lives.

'What about you, Sophia?'

'Hmm?' She looked up at him, blinking her surprise; she'd been so caught up in her depth of feeling she'd lost track of their conversation.

'Are you going to try and make amends with your family? To speak to them again?'

She gave a gentle sigh. 'I don't know. It's been so long since we talked properly, so long since… since we lost Amy. Maybe it's too late for us.'

'It's never too late, not while your parents are

still alive. I've told you before how much it would crush me to know Lily was somewhere in the world and scared of reaching out to me. To know that you and your parents have that separation because of something so tragic, something that none of you had any control over...'

He reached for her hand that she hadn't realised she'd clenched into a fist upon the table and slowly unravelled it to link his fingers through hers. 'You should try.'

She lowered her gaze to Lily, recalling her thoughts from seconds before, of her love for this child who wasn't even hers by birth, and she realised how right he was. She also realised the part she'd played in the breakdown of their relationship, the guilt she'd put on herself and projected onto them. She'd labelled herself as guilty and convinced herself that they blamed her too. She'd never given them a chance to prove to her otherwise; she'd never given them a chance to get close again.

She took a shaky breath and nodded. 'You're right.'

'I know I am.' He said it so sincerely that she couldn't even laugh at his arrogant acceptance of her words. 'And this trip is part of you facing up to your past with us by your side. If you can do this, you can do anything.'

She turned to him seconds before his head lowered to hers, his lips soft, gentle, as he kissed her.

It wasn't heated or desperate or needy; it was giving, the passion coming from the fact he cared for her, nothing more, nothing less, and she melted inside, her heart skipping to the beat of his choosing. The knowledge that she loved him was as obvious as the feelings projected in his kiss. She didn't just care for him, she wasn't just falling… She had long since fallen and as she opened her eyes and looked up into his she was convinced it was there, being reflected right back at her.

'Have faith in yourself,' he murmured as he pulled back and she smiled, leaning into him, her head coming to rest on his shoulder. It was comfortable, relaxed, and just where she belonged.

'I'll try.'

Jack turned and pressed his lips to Sophia's hair, breathing in the familiar scent of her shampoo and realised just how much he'd missed this. Missed her.

And seeing Lily so at home curled into her lap, to see the drawings spread out before him in all their hopeful glory… So much rested on this holiday, on him opening up to Sophia and being honest about how he felt, how, despite what he had said to the contrary, he had come to care for her… to love her.

Sophia nuzzled into him further, her head gradually getting heavy as her breathing levelled out and he smiled; she was falling asleep too.

He wrapped his arm around her, pulling her in close as he checked his watch. They would be landing soon but he could make the most of the next twenty minutes or so, before he'd have to wake them.

He looked back to the drawings on the table, spreading out the pages with his fingers until one in particular caught his eye...and his heart.

He lifted it out from beneath the pile and stilled, his chest both warm and tight. It was a church, in front of which stood a couple, and just like all the others, they were that couple. His dark skin, his dark hair, contrasted with Sophia's fair complexion and auburn waves, their hands locked together, a little Lily standing behind, her smile too big for her face. It was a wedding. *Their* wedding.

A conflicting sense of hope, fear and love swirled up within him, chased down by panic. Panic at Lily's obvious attachment and the fact that he had let it happen. Panic at his daughter's dream that this would be in their future and he couldn't say for certain that it would be. She'd already lost a mother. If he failed, if this relationship ended, she would lose another parental figure too.

Had he made a mistake?

He'd had the good sense to be cautious with Elena's mother, cautious about exposing Lily to that side of the family in case the relationship fell apart, in case she lost them. But his own connection to Sophia had made him rash.

Yes, they'd tried to keep things platonic in front of Lily, tried to show their relationship was one of friendship and nothing more. But this one picture told them they'd failed. That, regardless of their best efforts, Lily wanted Sophia to be a part of their family...just as he did.

He took a steadying breath and slid the picture back under the stack. He just had to make sure he didn't ruin it.

CHAPTER TWELVE

'PUT YOUR COATS ON,' Jack said, shrugging on his own as the engine to the plane was cut. 'It's going to be cold out there.'

Sophia helped Lily into hers before putting her own on, nerves fluttering up in her belly once more. This was it. Time to face her fears and move past them.

The door opened and the cold night air breached the warmth of the cabin, not that Lily was perturbed. She was already racing ahead, up to the elegant stewardess who now waited by the door for them to leave.

'Thank you for my pizza!'

'You're welcome, Miss McGregor.' The stewardess smiled indulgently down at Lily. 'Enjoy your holiday.'

'I will,' she said, stepping out onto the steps.

'Happy holiday, Mr McGregor, Miss Lambert.'

Sophia smiled her gratitude and stepped out behind Lily. The chilling wind, laced with snow, wrapped around her and she shivered, her hand reaching for Lily instinctively. 'Careful.'

'Isn't it pretty, Sphea?' the little girl said, her eyes wide with wonder as they travelled over the snow-banked airstrip. The darkness meant they couldn't see much further than the airfield, but Lily could see what she cared about and that was the snow.

Sophia swallowed past the wedge forming in her throat, pushing back the memories that threatened, barely noticing that Jack had come up alongside her until she felt the comforting warmth of his hand slipping around her own. She looked up at him, part fear, part gratitude, and the rest was all love shining in her gaze.

And she wasn't afraid to show it, not this time.

'Thank you for this, Jack.' She reached up on tiptoes and kissed his cheek. 'It means so much.'

'Thank you for coming.'

Their gazes locked, the air whipped around them, cold and frigid, but all she felt was the warmth of his gaze, heating her from the inside out and the hope flourishing with it. She couldn't remember a time when she'd been happier or felt more invincible.

It was strange when it all hinged on his feelings for her and they were entirely out of her control. Was it crazy? Or was it just a symptom of being in love?

And if it was the latter she was ready to get used to it.

What if he doesn't love you back? What if all this is a temporary affliction and in a week or two you have to go back to living as you did before?

She couldn't imagine it. She didn't want to.

'You okay?'

His question and the frown tugging at his brow halted her spiralling thoughts and she smiled. 'Never better.'

'Come on, Daddy, Sphea—can you save all the kissy-wissy stuff until later? I want to get to our bubble!'

Their eyes widened at Lily's astute observation and they each gave an awkward laugh.

'Patience, monkey.' Jack affectionately cuffed her chin, but Lily merely shook her head.

'Nuh-uh, it's my birthday trip!'

'She has a point,' Sophia said, feeling the guilt of it. Here she was, wrapped up in her own emotions, hers and Jack's, when this trip was all about Lily and giving her the best birthday possible.

She and Jack could wait—she looked back at him—they really could. She didn't want anything to get in the way of Lily's fun, least of all their romantic entanglement.

It had taken twenty-four years for her to meet the right man; she could at least wait four days before risking it by exposing the truth in her heart.

* * *

'Do you think she finally got over the fact that we're not sleeping in her bubble room tonight?' Jack asked Sophia as he sipped from the glass of wine in his hand and tried his hardest not to pull her to him, even though the urge had been with him ever since they'd put Lily to bed.

She smiled around her own glass, her eyes flickering with the flames of the roaring fire that bathed the suite's living area in its ambient glow, a striking contrast to the view beyond the glass. The floor-to-ceiling windows allowed for a seamless view over the Icelandic landscape, atmospheric and beautiful in its own cold, almost brutal way. The snowstorm that had hit shortly after they'd arrived continued to whip the flakes up into a frenzy and gave the impression of a life-size snow globe at work, blanketing the rugged hillside and making him glad they'd arrived before the worst of it.

'She was asleep before her head hit the pillow, and what a waste that would have been if we'd gone tonight. She'll realise that tomorrow.'

He nodded. 'True.'

'And it's hardly the weather for it,' she murmured, cupping her wine glass in her hands, the sleeves of her white high-neck jumper drawn into her palms and making her look far too sweet and vulnerable, and so utterly desirable. 'The forecast looks good for tomorrow though.'

'Hmm?' He'd been so caught up in her he'd missed the last.

'The forecast,' she said, one brow lifting, her eyes dancing. 'I said it looks better for tomorrow.'

He swallowed. 'Yes...yes, it does.'

He was finding it harder and harder to keep both his desire and his love for her in check, but he didn't feel ready to confess all. He had been, but that was before she'd accepted the offer of a separate hotel room.

Now he was starting to doubt so much and being uncertain wasn't an emotion he was accustomed to handling. In business and in his personal life, he depended on his steadfast control, his clear head, his ability to detach himself from the emotional and form decisions, take action based on facts.

With her, it was becoming nigh on impossible to remain detached and to trust his instincts, which he knew were clouded by his own feelings for her.

And the fact was she'd accepted the offer of another room.

He'd booked it while they were apart and he'd done it out of courtesy, wishing her to have the option. But the hope that she would turn it down and admit that she wished to stay with them had been there. It was still there.

'It's not really a hardship staying here either,' she said softly, her eyes sweeping the room, with its salvaged hardwood floors, sheepskin furs and glazed concrete walls. It was an eclectic mix of industrial chic and natural materials working together in harmony to give a sense of high-end luxury.

'You approve?'

'You asked me the same question on the plane...' Her eyes came back to him, her smile teasing.

'I know. Call me soft, but I care for your approval.'

She studied him quietly and he would have paid his fortune to know what was going through her mind. She wet her lips and leaned forward to place her glass on the coffee table formed from lava rock and rich wood.

'I should probably head back to my room.'

'What if I said I'd like you to stay?'

Even in the low light of the fire he could make out the flush of colour to her skin, the nervous flicker of her eyes as they came back to him. 'If I stay much longer I won't leave and then we'll have some explaining to do to Lily.'

Lily. Was that all she was worried about?

All? You should be worrying too.

But he didn't want her to leave.

'And you need to get some sleep too,' she pushed. 'When was the last time you slept?'

Truth was, he didn't know, not properly at any rate. 'I dozed on the plane from Tokyo.'

'That doesn't count.' Her eyes raked over his face and then he saw it. She was worried about Lily, but she was worried about him too.

'Do I look that bad?'

'Bad, no. Tired, yes.'

He raked a hand through his hair and took a breath. What would she say if she knew the reason was more down to her than the jet lag and all the travel put together? She occupied his mind day and night, keeping him alert, keeping him on edge as he wrestled with what he felt for her.

She surprised him by scooting over to him and cupping his cheek, her thumb grazing against his five o'clock shadow. 'You should take a leaf out of your daughter's book and admit defeat. Get some sleep. We have days ahead to enjoy and I don't want *us* getting in the way of Lily's birthday trip.'

And then she kissed him, her lips soft and gentle and a complete contrast to the fire coming alive inside. He wrapped his arm around her, pulling her close as he sought to deepen the kiss, to take all that she would give.

She was as breathless as he when she broke away, and in no way ready for sleep, but still she said, 'Goodnight, Jack.'

He reached for her hand as she rose. 'Don't go.'

She smiled down at him, releasing his hand slowly. 'I have to, and deep down you know that too.'

Did he? He gazed up at her, his eyes stinging

with the effort. He was too tired to analyse, too het up to worry about it; he just knew his instinct was to keep her close.

'Go to bed, Jack. Tomorrow's a new day.'

She pressed a kiss to his forehead and made for the door, looking back over her shoulder to say, 'Move before you fall asleep right there...'

And then she was gone and his eyes were closing, his glass tipping in his hand and acting as the wake-up call he needed.

Bed. She was right; he needed sleep. There would be time for them another night.

And this holiday was about Lily's birthday above all else, just as she'd reminded him, just as he should have remembered too.

Maybe he was more jet-lagged than he'd first realised...jet-lagged and in too deep...

He'd never felt more out of control in all his adult life. Entirely off balance. It was scary, unsettling and enough to have him moving to bed in the hope that tomorrow, after a decent sleep, he would at least have a better handle on it all.

CHAPTER THIRTEEN

'COME ON, DADDY, the car is waiting.'

Lily was hopping from one foot to the other, looking up at Jack imploringly and Sophia felt for her. This wasn't exactly the morning she'd had planned either, especially when today was her birthday.

The first full day of their trip and Lily's birthday breakfast had already been interrupted by a call from London that Jack just had to take and now, over an hour later, he was back on the phone again, dealing with the same issue. Some difficulty with some takeover or other. Not that Sophia could piece it together from the one half of the conversation she could hear but it had Jack scowling down the phone as they stood in the hotel lobby waiting for him to finish.

'Sorry, sweetheart...' he covered the bottom half of his phone as he spoke to her '... I'll be done soon.'

Lily looked to Sophia. 'Can we go outside and play in the snow?'

Sophia felt Jack's eyes shoot to her even as her skin prickled and her stomach twisted. She wet her lips and gave Lily a small smile. 'Let's just wait for Daddy; he won't be long.'

'Lily, just be patient,' he said, and Sophia gave him a grateful look for understanding, even as she felt foolish for her overreaction. She had agreed to come here; moreover, she'd witnessed an entire snowstorm last night and survived it. But going outside in daylight, surrounded by it…it was different.

Lily crossed her arms and gave a little huff.

'Hey, come on, he really won't be long.'

Lily didn't look convinced and if Sophia was honest she wasn't so sure he'd be done soon either since he was pacing back and forth in the lobby now, deeply engrossed.

A family of four chose that moment to come bustling into the lobby, a girl and boy not far off in age from Lily herself. The parents headed to Reception while the two kids laughed their way out of the big glass doors and kicked off a snowball fight just outside.

Lily watched them through the glass, the wistful look in her eye tugging at Sophia's heartstrings.

They moved off soon enough, a car rolling in to take them away, but that look was still in Lily's eye, her hand now pressed up against the glass as she stared out at the stark white landscape.

Sophia looked back to Jack, still pacing, and told herself to grow a pair. This was Lily's birthday trip; she should be more important than some business call. But then, what did she know about running a corporate empire? The leisure industry was bad enough. Maybe this was the way of things for him. It wasn't as if the business world stopped just because he was on holiday. And it was a Thursday after all, hardly the weekend.

'Okay, Lily, let's go play while we wait for your father.' She offered out a hand to her, which she took, her smile worth every nervous flutter.

Jack quit pacing. 'Where are you going?'

'Just out front; we can make a snowman while you finish your call.' She smiled down at Lily encouragingly. 'What do you reckon? Can we make one that looks like Daddy?'

Lily laughed. 'Yes!'

Jack wasn't smiling though. When she looked back to him his scowl seemed less about the call and more her suggestion.

'Don't worry; we'll be flattering,' she said, trying to lighten the sudden darkness in the room.

'I'd rather you stayed here.'

Sophia frowned. Seconds ago, she'd been convinced he was concerned for her, and how she'd feel playing out in the snow with a small child, and without him. But now...

Then she remembered the time on Samantha's doorstep when he'd told her with no hesitation that he wouldn't leave Lily at the party, how clear he'd been about not trusting her with just 'anyone,' and the reason he too had joined Lily for her sleepover ultimately.

But it couldn't be that now? Not after all they had shared, all that had happened between them. He had to trust her…didn't he?

'Please, Daddy.'

He looked to Sophia for backup, but she was too flummoxed and upset and confused, trying to convince herself it was because he was worried about her, even though she knew deep down it wasn't. Maybe it had been initially, but not now.

'We can stay just the other side of the glass,' she offered quietly, ignoring the way her skin now prickled, not with her phobia of the snow—or worse, being responsible for a child in the snow—but with his mistrust of her.

He looked from them to the glass and back again, his frown lifting a little. 'Okay—just keep where I can see you, agreed?'

'Agreed,' she said, now feeling like a child herself, anger sparking. She tugged Lily's hand gently, her death stare for him alone, not that he seemed to notice as his attention shifted back to the phone. 'Come on, birthday girl, let's go and have some fun.'

They went outside and she did as she'd promised, kept them close to the glass as they rolled the snow and built their man. With his bulbous belly and a Sophia-fist-sized punch hole for his mouth, two beady rocks for his eyes and a thin stone for his nose.

Lily stood back and laughed. 'It doesn't look much like Daddy, does it?'

Sophia had half a mind to storm back inside and pull his scarf off him just to wrap it around his icy counterpart and complete the look.

Still, in her anger, she'd forgotten all about her own trepidation…

Lily looked through the glass to where her father was pacing again, his scowl still present, his hand caught halfway through his hair. Sophia checked her watch. At this rate it would be dark before they even started their tour and whilst they would still hopefully get a glimpse of the northern lights when the sun disappeared, she'd like to see the waterfalls and the black sand beach in daylight.

She gave him a look through the glass, one which she hoped said, *Don't forget whose birthday it is*, and tapped her wrist, indicating the time. He grimaced and looked at his own, turning away a second to say something down the phone and then he cut the call and strode for the exit.

'Here he comes,' Sophia said, her hands falling to Lily's shoulders as she turned her to face the door and her father now coming through it.

'I'm so sorry, birthday girl.' He raced up to her and swung her up in the air. 'You ready?'

'Yes!' she squealed, her legs kicking excitedly and sending snow flying from her feet.

Sophia smiled at the heart-warming scene, her anger falling away as quickly as it had come. 'First you need to see our snow Daddy.'

Payback...

He looked at the snowman and back at her, slowly sliding Lily down his front until her feet were back on the ground.

'It's you, Daddy.'

'Me?' His eyes flitted from it, to Lily, to Sophia. 'And you think it's a true likeness?'

She eyed him as she pretended to consider both him and their creation. 'Seems pretty good, if you ask me.'

Lily laughed and Sophia grinned up at him. 'If only you'd been able to help, then maybe he'd have been a little less...portly.'

'Is that so?' he said, his eyes twinkling. 'I only have myself to blame then.'

'Precisely. Now, don't dilly-dally; the car has been waiting long enough.'

She turned on her heel and made her way to the slick chauffeur-driven four-by-four hired to navigate the tricky Icelandic terrain, leaving them to enjoy the view.

She knew he was watching her, and felt that kick of admiration in his gaze before she'd looked away. He liked that she stood up to him. Maybe he'd therefore welcome the idea already setting up camp in her brain that he should switch the pesky little mobile *off*.

'I *really* like Sphea, Daddy. Like really, really like her.'

Lily's words reached her and her lips quirked up, her heart fluttering in her chest. *I really, really like you too, kiddo.*

She couldn't hear Jack's response as the driver greeted her, opening up the rear door for her to climb in, but she hoped Jack's had been close to a ditto at least.

She settled into the back seat, watching them as they headed towards her, Jack's eyes locking with hers, assessing, searching. Was he looking for the anger he must have spied in her earlier?

She softened her gaze with a smile, which he readily returned. Fact was, she'd been mad—she was still mad when she thought on it—but she couldn't *stay* mad at him.

They got in beside her, Lily taking up the seat by the window so that she could enjoy every second of the passing landscape, which put Jack alongside her. Close—too close.

No, she couldn't stay mad, which was annoying and frustrating in its own way.

He looked at her, his eyes flitting from her lips to her eyes and back again, their intensity deepening into something else, something more primal and making her tummy contract over a rush of heat.

Not helping...

She looked away, to the back of the driver's head as he climbed into the car and demanded Jack's attention as they ran through that day's itinerary and the impact their two-hour delay had had. *Two hours.* All thanks to his blasted phone.

Jack was exhausted. Heaven knew whether he'd truly slept properly last night. She'd not had a chance to ask him since his phone had rung the second they'd sat down to breakfast. He needed a holiday, a real break. The thing had to go, and she'd speak to him about it the first chance she got.

As for the trust issue...that would be harder to raise. But maybe she'd just got it wrong. She looked to the passing landscape, the snow-capped rocks, the trees drooping under the weight of it all. It was pretty, even if it did coax memories to the fore that she would prefer remained buried.

Maybe it hadn't been his lack of trust in her to look after Lily at all; maybe she was being unfair and overly sensitive because she hadn't trusted herself either. She breathed through the rising knot of anxiety in her chest, flexing her tightened fists as she closed her eyes against the view, and then she felt his hand upon her knee.

She turned to see him looking down at her, the emotion blazing in his gaze reassuring her and letting her know he was there.

Yes, maybe she had been wrong, because if anyone deserved the benefit of the doubt it was him.

She rubbed her head against his shoulder, much like a cat would do to their owner's leg, and whispered, 'Thank you.'

He gave a soft laugh. 'So I'm forgiven.'

'For now.'

Jack's phone call had cost them two hours of daylight but his driver was a pro at navigating the terrain and facing off the aftermath of last night's storm. The sky was looking better by the hour which made that evening's stay all the more hopeful.

He'd wanted to book their holiday for longer— the longer the stay the more chance they would get a glimpse of the natural phenomena that they were here for, but he hadn't wanted to risk Sophia saying no and, as that morning's call proved, he needed to get back to work. But they were here now, and they could make the most of it.

He'd seen Sophia's face and known she was angry with him; he wanted to make it up to her, to both of them, and so far Iceland's impressive sights were winning it for him. They'd trekked around Seljalandsfoss waterfall, been awestruck by its immense drop and the roaring glacier waters. They'd stopped at Skógafoss, another immense waterfall which had earned a breathtaking smile from Sophia and a squeal from Lily when the sun had shone through the spray and produced a rainbow so vivid and colourful.

'It's Mummy!' Lily had turned to him and shouted.

And he'd had to smile, because she was right. The saying he'd always told his daughter was strong in her memory: *When it rains look for rainbows...when it's dark look for stars.*

He smiled as he remembered the pleasure in her face, what he could make out between her thick woolly hat and the scarf as high as her nose. The moment had been perfect and, he hoped, captured for ever in his little girl's memory.

They were back in the car now, heading for the last stop before their destination for the night. It was two in the afternoon, still time to catch it in daylight and get to their room for the night... Room. It really was just a room, with nothing but the woodland and the sky surrounding them. They'd all be in the one bed too, but he knew Sophia knew this. And yes, he knew nothing could happen, but he didn't care. The idea of them all being together under the stars was just so—

His phone started to ring, breaking the peaceful harmony in the car. Both Sophia and Lily sent him a look and he grimaced as he pulled it out of his pocket. Even the driver up front was giving him the evil eye through the rear-view mirror— at least that was how it felt.

He checked the screen: *Connor.*

He grimaced more. He had to take it. This take-over was becoming a royal pain in the prover-bial, but he wanted it. And he always got what he wanted...eventually.

Sophia looked to the screen too. 'Connor again? Is the guy so incapable of doing his job he has to keep ringing?'

Her remark smarted. Connor wasn't incapable. In fact, Connor was remarkable; he was two years his junior and yet he'd proved time and time again just how capable he was.

So why is he ringing you to talk through the latest issue?

He swiped the call to answer and gave a curt, 'What is it?'

Connor went straight into detail. He knew Jack's time was short, even shorter with him sup-posedly on holiday. He listened intently as his number two did his best to keep it brief, but it wasn't brief enough for Sophia. Her eyes kept slipping to him, her frown deepening with each second.

'Are you happy for me to proceed on that basis, Jack?'

Basis—what basis?

He realised his mind had wandered, too dis-tracted by Sophia's displeasure let alone his daughter's, and then he shook himself out of it. What was he even doing? He'd employed Connor years back. The guy had proved his worth over and over, and yet here he was, seeking his approval for another matter.

And then the truth hit him like a slap to the face. Connor was like that because *he'd* made him that way. *He'd* made him seek approval, *he'd* made him ensure that he was abreast of every situation, involved in every decision, *he'd* demanded that involvement instead of bestowing on him the trust his role demanded.

Jack was a fool, a prize idiot. He'd employed Connor to cover his absences, to be him in his absence, yet his controlling behaviour and his treatment of him had resulted in the complete opposite.

'Connor, stop.'

'I'm sorry… Was that not—?'

'No, Connor, I mean stop. I mean follow your instincts. I trust you to get this right.'

'You—*you* trust me?'

He could sense the guy's frown down the phone.

'Yes. I wouldn't have employed you otherwise. Do what you think you need to, get us this deal. I trust you to do what's right for the company.'

'And you?'

'I'm on holiday. Not to be disturbed until Monday at the earliest.'

'*Monday?*'

'Yes.'

'Right. Okay. No problem, I'm on it.'

'I know you are.'

'Thank you, Jack.'

'I think it will be me thanking you next week, Connor.'

He could sense his number two smiling now as Jack cut the call and looked from one lady to the other. 'Happy?'

'Yes!' they both piped up and he took a gloved hand from each and gave them a squeeze. Content, happy, relaxed…and so very tired. But that could wait. He'd get some sleep tonight. He had a feeling this was a turning point for him—changing his work-life balance and putting his faith in others.

He thought back to that morning and the fear that had gripped him at the idea of Sophia and Lily venturing out alone. No. He wasn't ready for that. A foreign country, the two people who meant most to him in the world. No. Leaving his company in Connor's hands was fine. Acceptable even. But letting these two out of his sight in a country he didn't know. No. Just no.

He gripped their hands tighter, his love for them overriding.

'Thank you for doing that,' Sophia suddenly said into the quiet.

'It's long overdue.'

'Yes,' she said, the vehemence in her voice surprising him. 'Even if it wasn't Lily's birthday, I'd say the same. Everyone needs time off once in a while. Even someone as successful and as invincible as you.'

Invincible? He didn't feel invincible right now with her eyes looking up at him, their sheen, their concern killing him inside.

'I know,' was all he could manage as he fought back the urge to kiss her.

'Good.'

She wet her lips, her eyes scanning his face, and he realised the urge existed within her too and it was enough. Just to know they shared that need, that she cared for him enough to state her approval of his decision. It was enough.

'We are here, Mr McGregor.'

The Reynisfjara black sand beach was unlike anything she'd ever seen before. Not difficult considering she'd barely travelled out of the UK. Even when she'd attended the training courses put on by her company abroad, she'd kept close to the hotel studying, connecting, networking.

And oh, my, how different things are now...

It wasn't just her travel status changing, it was her whole outlook on life, on what was truly important and what really made her happy. How was it possible for so much to change in such a short space of time?

She pulled her gaze from the waves crashing at the base of the rugged basalt stacks out at sea and looked to Jack. She knew the answer well enough. Even with his woollen hat and his scarf wrapped high around his face leaving her with just a glimpse of his sparkling grey eyes, he made her tummy flutter and her heart warm. At his side was Lily, a perfect miniature copy with her curls escaping her hat, her eyes as grey as his, peering out above the edge of her scarf.

It was the two of them who made her keen to do what she could to repair her relationship with her mum and dad. They made her want more out of life, more than just work.

They were studying the grey basalt columns rising out of the black sand, Jack leaning down to listen to his daughter above the roar of the sea, and she smiled. Lily was likely telling him all about their formation, from lava to volcanic rock… He really hadn't been lying when he'd said she'd been absorbing every word of the brochure. And Sophia couldn't be happier to see the delight in Lily's face at every landmark they visited.

It was the perfect birthday, with or without Aurora playing ball tonight, ever more so to know that even now Jack's phone was turned off in his jacket. He'd taken it out as soon as they'd stepped out of the car and Lily and Sophia had both glared at it. But he'd simply smiled and declared he was turning it off, saying that all those he cared about were right here with him and that no emergency would be important enough to change that.

It had warmed her top to toe, just as it did now. She'd loved to think…she wanted to think…he'd included her in that sweeping comment, but as much as she now knew she loved him, she had to keep her hope under control.

'So, birthday girl,' Jack said, clapping his hands together, 'are you ready to head to our bubble for the night?'

Lily looked up at him, her gloved hand tugging her scarf away from her mouth. 'Yes!'

'Great. Dinner first, though, then bubble.'

She pouted.

'What—you must be hungry? Aren't you hungry, Sophia?'

'We could grab a picnic?'

'Oh, yes!' Lily blurted. 'A picnic under the stars!'

'Aren't you full of great ideas?' he teased, his eyes dancing into hers and making her come alive inside, heat, laughter and happiness all bubbling up. 'I'll arrange for our food to meet us there… Does mean I'll be needing this though…'

He pulled out his phone and they both grinned.

'For food, we can forgive you, Daddy.' Then she hooked her hands in Sophia's and Jack's, tugging them back towards the car. 'Hurry—the sky is still clear… I have a really good feeling in my… what is it Ms Archer says—*waters*?'

They all laughed. And, truth was, Sophia had a good feeling too. But it was less about the sky and more about her companions. Her smile behind her scarf grew, her cheeks aching from the effort. She'd never smiled so much before that it hurt; she hadn't even known it possible. Not before the McGregors, before her life had started to feel so complete…

Jack knew of camping, glamping, caravanning… you name it, he knew of it…but never had he done such a thing.

He stared up at the roof of their bubble for the night and seriously wondered whether he'd lost his mind. It wasn't that there was just the one room, the one bed even, it was the fact that a toilet trip required a dash into the depths of the forest, in the freezing snow with a torch for company. Plus, he was exhausted—all the fresh air, the lack of decent sleep these last few weeks and now…*this*.

'Isn't it amazing?' Lily's voice was breathless with wonder as she twirled on the spot beside him, her head back, her eyes on the darkening sky above.

He looked at the obvious pleasure in her face and forgot every negative thought. This was why he'd booked it. He could have booked a luxury lodge, a glass-framed house, anything but a solitary bubble in the middle of a forest, but this was what Lily wanted. A true experience under the stars with them all in one bed together, and he had to admit, after spending last night apart from Sophia, the idea of it made any amount of 'slumming it' worth it.

'We'd best eat before you get too distracted,'

Sophia teased Lily as she rummaged through the bags of food that had been delivered and started to lay out a feast on the bed. Hams, cheeses, breads, fruit…more continental breakfast than evening dinner in Jack's eyes, but so long as the women were happy.

Who was he kidding?

He was happy. As they sat on the bed munching away, their chatter so easy and comfortable, he was happier than he'd ever been. Happier than he'd even known possible, and he knew the cause was sitting right opposite him, her cheeks glowing in the soft light given off by the solitary lantern, her eyes bright and often locking with his, the hint of a smile permanently on her lips, save for when she was laughing and then her whole face lifted, the mood in the bubble right along with it.

'Can we turn the light off now?' Lily pleaded, pushing her plate away and trying to settle back on the bed.

'Let me just get rid of these…' Sophia started to clear everything away and he moved to help her, their hands colliding over the same dish. She smiled up at him, he smiled back, the connection holding them captive.

'Ahem!' Their eyes snapped to a stern-looking Lily, a giggle erupting from them both as she crossed her arms over her chest. 'No kissing allowed.'

'I wasn't.'

'I didn't.'

They both said in unison.

The little girl raised her brow in total disbelief and Jack looked back at Sophia. 'Well, I may have thought about it.'

Sophia laughed and pulled away, taking the piled-up plates with her and flicking off the light.

'Oh, wow!' It came from Lily, but Jack was thinking it, his eyes now lost to the skies above as he lay back beside his daughter and took it all in.

It was majestic, ethereal, out of this world. Stars glittered as far as the eye could see, and swirling arcs of mist-like patterns streaked across the sky, casting an almost eerie glow.

'I feel like I'm in a dream,' Lily said as Sophia lay down next to her, the three of them now in a row. He felt Lily take his hand, saw her take hold of Sophia's too and pull them both onto her chest. 'It's perfect. This is perfect.'

It was. The perfect everything. And surprisingly comfy. He could already feel his body winding down, his eyes growing heavy as he worked his shoulders into the cushiony softness beneath him. He yawned and blinked rapidly, staving off sleep.

'You should make a wish,' Sophia murmured. 'With all those stars above, it has the greatest chance of coming true.'

'I will,' Lily said with a bob of her head, her small hands squeezing at them both.

He turned his head to look at his daughter, watching her close her eyes, her face screwed up in concentration, and then she opened them. 'Done.'

'What did you wish for?' he asked, his eyes catching Sophia's over Lily's head and knowing what he would wish for if he were six again and he'd lived a life where he could believe in such things. He'd make a wish for the thirty-year-old him, a wish likely to be very similar to Lily's.

'I can't tell you that, Daddy. It won't come true if I do.'

'Of course, how silly of me.' He smiled at her, his eyes lifting back to Sophia's and pausing just long enough to let her know his own wish and hoping she too could share it.

'Thank you for the best birthday.'

'It was all Sophia's doing.'

'I know—I *was* thanking her.' And then she laughed and pressed a kiss to his cheek. Turned to give one to Sophia too. Then she lay back and they all stared up at the sky, absorbing the natural beauty Earth had to offer and forgetting how imperfect life could be.

CHAPTER FOURTEEN

'I'M READY!'

Lily's call came from her bedroom just as Jack entered the living area with a glass of wine for her. It was their last night in Iceland and they were back in the hotel suite Jack had booked for the first night. Tomorrow they would be back in the UK and then…and then what?

She smiled to hide her worry and took it from him. 'Thanks.'

'I'll go and get her settled, won't be long.'

She nodded and watched him go, her thoughts no less troubled. They hadn't discussed the future, and Sophia still didn't feel ready to confuse Lily's birthday trip with it. But everything he did, everything he said—it all indicated that he was starting to feel the same.

And the more time she spent with him, the more they shared, the more *I love you* threatened to erupt.

Here's your food, Sophia.

I love you.

Here's your drink, Sophia.
I love you.
I'll get the door, Sophia.
I love you.

She shook her head at her own madness and settled into the couch, enjoying the soothing quality of the wine and the warming fire.

'Hey, Sophia.' He leaned his head around the corner. 'She's asking for you too.'

He gave an apologetic smile and she grinned back, unfolding herself from the sofa and leaving her glass on the table as she joined him.

'It's no problem. I'd like to anyway.' She moved to walk past him and he reached out, his hand gentle on her arm to stop her.

'Sophia?'

'Yes.' She looked up into the warmth in his gaze and felt it again, ever more pressing, ever more urgent… *I love you.*

'Please stay tonight—with us, with me?'

Her heart squeezed in her chest, her body stiffened. 'I…' The refusal died on her lips. She didn't want to leave.

'Please?' He pressed again and she felt her shoulders ease, her heart too. It was what she wanted.

'Yes.'

He pulled her to him, the heat of his body permeating their jumpers, his scent assailing her senses. 'You will?' he rasped.

She nodded, her eyes falling to his lips, and then he kissed her and any remaining doubt ebbed away on a flurry of heat and happiness.

He broke away too soon for her body's liking. 'Sorry, I just had to do that.'

And she could only smile as he took her hand and led her into Lily's room.

She was already in bed, the pillow up behind her, Baby Bear on her belly with her favourite book open and ready.

They climbed in, one on each side, and she looked from one to the other, her grin quite satisfied.

'Happy?' Jack said to her.

'Yes, now I am. Aren't we, Baby Bear?'

Sophia could feel Jack's gaze on her, feel her own lips lift with a happiness she couldn't contain.

'You read, Sphea.' Lily edged the book closer to her and snuggled in. 'You can be my new mummy, can't you?'

Her eyes shot to Jack's, catching his sudden pallor and...*what*—panic?

'I don't think anyone can replace your mummy, darling.'

'No, but I can have two mummies. People do, don't they? I've seen it on TV.'

Sophia's body relaxed a little, but Jack still looked like he'd seen a ghost.

'True, very true,' she said, kissing the little girl's head and starting to read, hoping Jack would relax and Lily would be satisfied with her non-answer. This was what she'd been worrying about—Lily's attachment, the what-if of it not working out, and having seen Jack's face…

But he'd wanted her to stay with him tonight. Surely that meant he wanted more?

More what though? A relationship? Or sex? Was she just filling a hole in that part of his life? He'd been clear about his feelings towards Elena, his inability to love before.

Had she really just been so blinded by her own love?

Her stomach twisted, her throat closing over and straining her voice as she tried to read.

Lily yawned. 'Daddy's turn now.'

She looked to Jack, but his attention was on the foot of the bed, distant, wary.

'Daddy?' Lily nudged him and his eyes snapped to her.

'What, monkey?'

'Your turn.' She passed him the book.

'Ah…okay.' He gave Sophia a quick look, a flicker of something in his gaze, and then his focus was on the book, his voice far more jovial than she knew he felt.

She should slip away now. Before he could hold her to her promise to stay. She started to move off the bed and felt his hand close around her own.

'Stay, please.'

She looked back into his face and in that second

she would have done anything he asked, because there was that look in his eye, the look she had come to depend on, the look that said he cared. Even if it wasn't love, it was enough to keep her there, for now.

She settled back down and he pulled his arm around her and Lily, his hand coming to rest on Sophia's shoulder, his thumb gently caressing her skin. He had to care for her.

He had to.

'Sophia…?'

They were walking through the corridor that led from Lily's bedroom to the living area, Sophia in front, him behind, and every part of him just wanted to reach out for her and pull her in. But he could sense she was trying to keep some distance. The fact she was walking ahead without even a backward glance was enough to tell him that.

'Sophia?' he tried again as she reached the sofa and lifted her glass from the table.

Slowly she took a sip and turned to look at him. The fire was no longer lit and the room was dark save for a solitary lamp and it cast a shadow over her face and made her look…sad.

He'd seen her look many things this holiday but that wasn't one of them. 'What is it?'

She shook her head and gave a small laugh, but it was shaky, unsteady. 'I don't know where to start.'

'You can tell me anything…' He stepped closer, pausing when he was a stride away. 'Is it me? Is it what Lily said?'

'It was your reaction when she said it…' She took a breath and it shuddered out of her. 'Look, I'm sorry, I don't want to hurt her. I don't want to come and go from her life like she doesn't mean anything to me.'

'I don't want you to either.'

'But I will if this, whatever this is, doesn't work out.'

'Do you want us to work out?'

She gave a gentle sigh. 'How can you ask me that?'

'It's a simple question, Sophia. Do you want there to be a you and me?'

She wet her lips, her eyes dark in the low light and glistening now. 'I'm a realist, Jack. It doesn't matter how swept away I get by you, by Lily, by all this…' She fluttered a hand around her. 'I can't help but think it will all get taken away.'

'It won't if we don't want it to.'

'But your face when Lily asked…when she asked about me being…you know…'

He shook his head, one hand reaching out for her, his palm soft upon her cheek. 'I felt guilty. I told you before I couldn't love Elena, not as she wanted me to, and she was her mother. She, of all people…'

He closed his eyes and breathed in deeply. He'd

never admitted so much to another person, never made himself vulnerable in this way before, but he knew he owed her this. The truth.

He opened his eyes and cupped her other cheek, cradling her face in his palms as he stepped forward to close the remaining distance between them. 'But you, Sophia, you make me feel that way.'

Her eyes shone up at him, her lips parting on an unspoken thought.

'When I'm not with you I think of you,' he whispered, 'and when I am I feel like I've come home, that I'm where I belong. I've never known the kind of happiness I've found by your side.'

'But…' She shook her head, the move so small he barely felt it. 'What are you saying, Jack?'

'Isn't it obvious?' He searched her eyes for what he wanted to see, desperately hoping she felt the same.

'No…'

'I'm in love with you, Sophia.'

She inhaled softly, her lashes fluttering as emotions flickered in the wide pools of her blue eyes, their colour so mesmerising, so familiar now that he could close his eyes and still they would be there, ingrained in his memory.

'And though it makes me feel guilty and vulnerable and in all manner of ways uncomfortable, I can't deny that I love you.'

'Is this really happening?' She trembled in his hands, her voice hushed.

'Believe it.' He kissed her, wanting her to feel it, wanting her to take his words and claim them for her own. 'Please believe it.'

He scooped her up in his arms, pressing another kiss to her lips. 'Let me show you how much I love you…'

He walked her to his bedroom and laid her down on the bed. Her eyes were unblinking as they followed him around the room, closing the door, turning the lights down low and stripping away his clothes.

'Jack…'

He paused over the button to his trousers. 'Yes?'

'I love you too.'

Her voice was so definite, so very real, and he stripped the last of his clothing in one swift motion, joining her on the bed and claiming her lips with his.

This was what coming home felt like. This was what love felt like. And now he'd found it he had no idea how he'd live without it again.

And if life was kind he would never have to.

CHAPTER FIFTEEN

SOPHIA STILL COULDN'T believe the night's events.

The sun wasn't even up and she was lying awake, Jack's arm across her naked tummy, his even breath brushing over her shoulder as he slept so deeply, so soundly. She knew how tired he was, the travelling having taken its toll, no matter how he tried to fight it, and she felt for him.

But this was a new beginning. They were talking about a future—a future in which Lily and Jack would settle in the UK. Less travel, more stability for Lily, more time for them—the three of them. It was all coming true and she was too abuzz to sleep any more.

The second she'd awoken she'd replayed his words of love, his attentive mouth as he'd travelled the length of her body, demonstrating his love for her in such a way that she had felt worshipped, cherished, loved more than she'd ever thought possible.

He loved her. He truly loved her.

And she was so utterly besotted, with him and Lily.

Life truly could be perfect. She'd never dared to believe, but now she did.

She turned to look at him beside her, felt that love blossom in her chest, her heart feeling so big it was impossible to breathe.

'I love you, Jack,' she whispered, and then she heard it, the sound of movement in the hallway. Lily was awake.

She frowned and strained to listen. Maybe she'd been mistaken. But no, there was the delicate patter of small feet, a brush of clothing against the wall.

Although Lily knew of their relationship— that ship had definitely sailed—she wasn't quite ready to have her walk in on them naked and entwined.

She slipped out from beneath Jack's arm and picked up her clothes from the floor, from where Jack had hastily deposited them. Her cheeks flushed even now at the memory and she pressed a hand to them, taking a cooling breath as she pulled them on and silently slid from the room.

She found Lily in the living area, her tiny frame dwarfed by the tall glass that currently showcased Aurora and the stars. It wasn't quite as striking as in their bubble, but it was no less mesmerising, and Lily was certainly mesmerised.

'Lily,' she whispered, not wanting to startle her.

She turned to her and smiled. 'Hi, Sphea.'

Sophia pressed a finger to her lips and gave a gentle, 'Shh, your daddy is sleeping.'

She nodded and looked back to the glass.

'I wish we didn't have to leave,' she murmured as Sophia joined her, her voice taking on a sad edge.

'You and me both,' Sophia admitted truthfully. 'But you know the weather is set to turn. There's another storm on the way and the hotel is already preparing for it. If we don't leave now, we might get stuck.'

'I wouldn't mind being stuck,' she said, looking up at her and taking hold of her hand.

Sophia gave her hand a little squeeze. 'I bet.'

'Do you think we could build another snowman before we go?'

'If we have time after breakfast, I'm sure we—'

'No, now. Just me and you.'

'I don't know, Lily…' She looked back towards the bedroom then the clock on the wall. It wasn't the dead of night, but it was hardly breakfast time either, and what if Jack woke and they weren't here?

'We could leave a note on the pillow; that way Daddy'll know where we are,' she said, guessing at the cause of Sophia's hesitation. 'And we don't want to wake him. He needs his sleep. He doesn't sleep enough.'

Sophia shook her head. 'When did you get so grown-up?'

She shrugged. 'He works too hard and travels too much…but hopefully that will all be different now.'

Her words chimed with Sophia's own hope for the future, for everything they'd yet to discuss but she felt in her heart would happen.

'I hope so too.'

'So can we? One last snowman and maybe a small walk, just to the lake?' Her eyes were wide and pleading and she couldn't say no, she just couldn't.

'Okay, get yourself dressed in warm clothing. I'll go and write the note.'

Lily gave a silent squeal, her hands tight on Sophia's, and then she was running, her tiny feet silent against the wooden floor as she made for her bedroom to get dressed.

Sophia shook her head, her smile so indulgent and full of love. If she could bottle happiness, she'd bottle this right now and make millions.

Only her man already had his own wealth, the happiness and the money and the love.

She shook her head some more as she made her way to the desk to seek out some paper and a pen.

She'd just finished placing the note on her pillow when she heard Lily's soft approach. She looked up to see her in the doorway, hat and gloves in hand, hair still ruffled from sleep. She smiled and placed a finger over her lips, gesturing to a sleeping Jack as she passed by the bed. Lily grinned and nodded.

She paused at the door and gave him one last loving look. 'Back soon, sleepyhead.'

They pulled on their hats and gloves and zipped their coats high as they made their way to the ground floor, passing the skeleton staff on the way with a respectful greeting and a smile. It did feel a little weird to be wandering around before sunrise, but she figured with a skyline like Iceland's they must be used to people heading out at all hours, looking to enjoy the view.

When they reached the main exit, Lily slipped her hand in hers. 'This is really exciting!'

'It is, isn't it.'

And it really was—her tummy danced with it. She wasn't sure whether it was the early hour, the magic of the lights continuing to ripple through the sky or the after-effects of last night, but she could feel it too. The butterflies, the excitement, the thrill of what was to come.

Jack woke to nothing. No noise. No Sophia. Nothing.

Instead of her warm, pliant body, he had her pillow clutched to his chest, her scent still there but no residual heat, no her. How long had she been gone?

He shoved it away, blinking against the chilling grey light that peeped through the gap in the blind, and the feeling of unease grew. The sun was up and yet there was no sound from Lily, no sound at all. She wouldn't sleep this late, even when jet-lagged; she was always up at the crack of dawn.

He raked a hand through his hair and over his face. He felt drugged, his head thick with too much sleep and it didn't help his unease. He threw back the covers and rose up, his head spinning with the speed of the move. One glass of wine and he felt like this…though it wasn't the wine. It wasn't even the persistent jet lag. It was the fact she had gone. That after the night they had shared she'd sneaked out without so much as a wake-up kiss.

But maybe he was wrong, maybe his ears were deceiving him, maybe she was in the living area keeping quiet to let him sleep. She knew how tired he'd been and it was just the sort of caring thing she would do.

He tugged on a pair of lounge pants, his feet heavy as he made for the doorway, and breathed in deep, his arms stretching out. Yes, she would be here, and if not here, maybe back in her own room getting ready for breakfast.

He looked through the gap in Lily's door. Her quilt was thrown back, her bed empty. He opened the door further. No sign. He carried on through the suite.

'Hello?'

Nothing.

'Lily… Sophia…'

Nothing.

A chill shot through him, his pace picking up. He got to the living area. Nothing. He turned and checked the bathrooms, the bedrooms again, every last possible space. Nothing.

Where were they?

Breakfast. Maybe they'd gone down to breakfast… *Without you?*

He tried to slow his stride, tried to calm his pulse. There was no need to panic. No need at all.

His mind travelled back three years, to his house all empty, to the plates on the table untouched, to the deathly sound of silence… He shook his head, shaking off the memory, and his voice was gruff as he sought to fill the quiet. 'You're overreacting.'

And still his skin prickled up, nausea swelling with the haunting past. He pulled on his clothes, his hands trembling with the sickening fear and slowing his progress.

'Just take it easy.'

Finally clothed, he grabbed his mobile, the room card and left, his pace picking up once more as he headed for Sophia's room. Maybe she'd taken Lily with her while he slept. Maybe she'd wanted to make sure he was undisturbed. *Yes*, perfectly reasonable.

He knocked on her door. He knocked again. Nothing.

Breakfast. They must be at breakfast.

He made his way downstairs, noting the staff rushing around, a stream of guests flooding the foyer.

'What's happening?' he asked one of the men, who was shucking his coat and shaking it out.

'Our tour had to turn back. The storm's heading this way and it's pretty nasty. Even managed to blow rocks into the car in front of us. Took it right off the road. Luckily no one was hurt.'

He saw the TV screen in the lobby showing the news report with the snowstorm warning, and the hotel staff were putting up signs warning guests against venturing out.

He swallowed. They wouldn't be out there. They'd be in the restaurant.

But the niggle inside wouldn't quit.

He looked through the glass to the looming skies fast approaching.

'Believe me, it's as nasty as it looks,' the guy said, spying his focus.

'Yeah,' Jack said, his voice sounding distant even to his own ears as his blood pounded over it. He turned away and headed to the restaurant, almost running.

Please be there, please, please...

'Just one more snowball?' Lily pleaded, her eyes alive with laughter, making Sophia shake her head indulgently.

'Just one, *please*.'

Just one...one more push...

Sophia clutched her stomach as it rolled with the memory. So vivid, so real, as if she was there now and it wasn't Lily she was seeing, it was Amy, begging her for that last sleigh ride, the last...

She swallowed and closed her eyes as if it would somehow push the image away.

Amy is gone—you can't change that. It wasn't your fault—it wasn't.

It was Jack's voice talking to her, soothing her, telling her to put the past to bed, and she felt his comfort as though he were there with her.

'Sphea? *Sphea?*'

She opened her eyes. Poor Lily's eyes were narrowed, concerned, her gloved hand reaching up to cover her own. 'What's wrong?'

She slipped her hand over Lily's and gave her a smile. 'Nothing, darling. I was just a little sad for a second.'

'We don't have to throw more snowballs.'

Sophia gave a soft laugh. 'It's not that, but we do need to be getting back. We don't want your dad worrying about where we've got to, especially with the weather already on the turn.'

It was true that the wind was whipping up, the sky hinting at the approaching storm, but as she looked from it to Lily she could see she wasn't reassured.

'You looked sad, Sphea. *Really* sad.'

'It was a sad memory that came back to me.'

'What was it?'

Lily's frown persisted, her loving eyes determined to get the truth out of her.

'It's a long story.'

'I like stories.'

'Not this one, darling.'

'I can take it. I'm a big girl!'

She pulled Lily in for a hug, more for her own reassurance than Lily's. 'I know you are...'

She inhaled softly, her mind remembering Amy in all her young and determined vibrancy, much like Lily's, and she tried to work out a way to tell her that was child-friendly and not too upsetting. She knew part of the battle was dealing with her own upset and not relaying that onto Lily more than she already had done.

And you should talk about Amy. You loved her. She was your sister. She doesn't deserve to be pushed out.

Her lips lifted a little with the thought. It was the most rational, most loving reason in the world to talk about her sister, and it had taken Jack talking sense into her for her to realise it.

The accident had been tragic, and she needed to tell Lily that she'd lost her, but she could also tell Lily just how amazing her sister had been, how special to her she was...

'I had a sister and her name was Amy...'

* * *

They weren't there. They weren't anywhere.

And he knew, even before he went to Reception to make enquiries, that they were outside somewhere, heaven knew where.

The receptionist who'd been on the desk to check them in the previous day smiled up at him as he approached, her smile morphing into a frown by the time he stood over her and she could read the worry in his face.

'Have you seen my daughter and…and…' What did he say? His girlfriend—the woman who had taken it upon herself to go out with a storm approaching, taking his daughter with her? 'The woman who travelled with us?'

'I'm afraid I haven't, sir. I've only just started my shift. Let me check with my colleagues.'

He nodded swiftly. 'Thank you.'

She moved from behind the desk and walked into a room behind Reception. He turned on the spot, scanning all the people, outside and in. People bustled about, prepping for the storm, guests milled about, working out revised plans for the day, but no Lily, no Sophia.

The receptionist returned. 'It seems they went out about an hour or so ago.'

'Out?' His throat tightened around the word as his worst fears were confirmed and he had to swallow to ask, 'Did they say where they were heading?'

'I'm afraid not, sir, but…well, no one asked.'

Of course they hadn't. Why would they? He raked his hands through his hair, took a steadying breath—*think, think…*

'Did anyone see which way they went?'

Her frown deepened, her head shaking. 'But I'm sure they will be back very soon. The storm is picking up and—'

'Cameras? Do you have cameras out front?'

'Well, yes…'

'Can you check the footage, tell me which way they headed?'

'Of course, sir. I'll ask Security right away, but I don't think you should be—'

'Thank you,' he said over her. He wasn't interested in her advice. No one, no storm, would stop him looking for them.

He looked to the glass, to the wind whipping through the trees, the snowfall starting to build and adding to the thick layer already down. Despite the staff's best efforts, even the path out front, the drive to it too, were no longer visible between the high banks of snow.

He started to pace. He couldn't take this much longer. He needed to get out there, start looking. What if the worst were to happen? What if it already had?

'Sir?'

His eyes shot to the desk, to the woman looking up at him, apprehensive now. 'They headed towards the lake.'

'The lake?' he choked out.

'Yes, sir.'

The lake was through the woods, down a steep bank. It would be slippery, iced over… He was already striding for it.

'Sir, you shouldn't. You—'

He wasn't listening. Instinct fired in his blood, drove his limbs, his mind… He couldn't go through this again—he couldn't.

As they cleared the bank and the woods the snowstorm really made itself known, the trees no longer sparing them the worst of it.

'It's lucky we left when we did!' she yelled over the wind at Lily, whose hand was clutched in hers.

Lily nodded but said nothing. It was hard to talk with the snow lashing against their faces, biting into the band of skin left exposed between their hats and scarves, their eyes struggling to stay open.

She tugged Lily closer and leaned forward against it, her head bowed.

'Sophia!'

Jack?

She lifted her head, blinking as she tried to focus. There was a shape in the distance, coming towards them. The closer they trudged, the more she could see. It was him. And…and he wasn't even wearing a coat. She cursed inwardly—*what on earth?*

A sense of foreboding had the icy chill spreading on the inside now, her skin breaking out in a fevered sweat.

'Lily!' His yell was harsh, choked even. *Oh, no…*

'What's Daddy doing?' Lily shouted up at her.

'I've no idea. Come on.'

She tried to quicken their pace but the snow had banked fast and it was almost as high as Lily's legs. She turned into the little girl and picked her up, wrapping her legs right around her as she continued on. But Jack was faster. He was suddenly upon them, his arms reaching out for Lily and pulling her from Sophia.

She looked up and saw everything she feared looking back at her. His eyes were wide, a terrified sheen covering his dark skin. *'Jack?'*

He shook his head, his eyes blazing as the snow fell thick and fast around them. 'Inside. Now.'

Even Lily knew better than to say anything, but she looked at Sophia over his shoulder, her frown forming anew. She knew something was wrong. Something was *very* wrong.

Sophia followed on autopilot, her heart racing in her chest, her gut plummeting. Was this all because she had taken Lily out? Alone? Without him?

She remembered all the times she had questioned his trust in those around him, his trust in her, and she knew it to be true.

He'd said he loved her. He'd told her he loved her less than twelve hours ago.

But if he loved her, truly loved her as she did him, how could he not trust her?

She followed blindly, her thoughts spiralling out of control, her heart rate too. Everything had been so perfect, so right…and now…now she realised it was all a lie.

No, not a lie. She'd believed him when he'd said he loved her. But hadn't he also said he wasn't capable of loving anyone the way they deserved? And wasn't that exactly what this proved?

She'd been a fool. A fool to believe this was possible. A fool to believe she deserved her own happy-ever-after.

A fool to fall in love and believe she'd be loved in return.

Because what was love without trust?

Not enough.

He knew Sophia followed him. He was as attuned to her footfall as he was to Lily's living, breathing form in his arms, past and present colliding with sickening clarity. Only Lily was bigger, much bigger now, and Sophia…she wasn't Elena.

He opened the door to his suite and strode in. Her footsteps ceased. 'Come in, Sophia.'

He couldn't look at her. Instead he headed for Lily's room; he needed her warm and very, very safe.

'Daddy, why are you mad?' Lily lifted her head off his shoulder, the concern in her gaze crushing him.

'I'm not mad. I was worried.'

'Because we were gone?'

He nodded and lowered her to her feet.

'But we left you a note…'

'A note?'

He crouched, his hands sweeping over her face, her hair, taking off her hat as he kissed her forehead and held her face close.

'Uh-huh.' She nodded. 'On the pillow, next to you.'

He dragged in a breath. So he'd missed the note. It was likely wrapped up in the bed sheets. It didn't change what had happened, how close they'd been to putting themselves in danger.

'You get yourself into some dry clothes, okay? I'm just going to talk to Sophia.'

'Don't be mad with her. It was my fault. I begged her to take me out.'

He closed his eyes and kissed her once more. 'Off you go.'

She nodded but he could tell she wanted to say more…so much more…and he didn't want to hear it. He rose up and closed her door, turning back to see Sophia still on the threshold, her hat and gloves clutched to her chest, her eyes averted and skin pale.

'What did you think you were doing?'

She started like a frightened rabbit, her eyes coming to him, wide and glinting. 'She wanted to play in the snow just one last time before…before we left.'

He stalked towards her, his anger fizzing in his bloodstream. 'And you thought that was wise, with a storm on its way?'

He threw a hand in the direction of the outdoors, shaking his head in disbelief. 'Anything could have happened, Sophia. *Anything.*'

'It was…it was f-fine when we left. The sky was virtually clear, the lights were dancing, and Lily… Lily just wanted to play some more in the snow.'

'At the lake! You, of all people, should know better than that!'

He was shaking inside and out as he loomed before her now. He couldn't stop. He was so afraid, so angry. He needed her to see what she had done, to realise the danger in it. If he had lost Lily— *hell*, if he had lost Sophia too… And she looked so tiny right now, so fragile and easily broken, her auburn hair a crazy mess around her porcelain complexion.

He reached for her, gripping her forearms, grateful that she was living and breathing in his hold even as the words tumbled out of him. 'What if you'd fallen, what if she'd slipped, what if you'd cracked your head open on a rock, then what? What would have happened?'

She inhaled sharply, her eyes widening, the tears quick to well. 'How could you say that to me?'

He stared at her, saw the hurt in her eyes, the pain, the anguish, and his stomach lurched. She wasn't seeing him; she was seeing the death of her sister all over again. After all he'd said, after he'd encouraged her to move on, to believe she wasn't to blame.

'Sophia…' He cursed, squeezing his eyes shut and opened them again, his head shaking. 'I didn't mean…'

She pulled out of his grasp, stepping backward, her own head shaking, the tears spilling over. 'You meant it.'

'Sophia, I just… I couldn't go there again, after Elena, after she'd run out…the accident… I have to keep Lily safe…and you, you were out there…'

She was still shaking her head, her whole body trembling. 'You *told me* it wasn't my fault. You *told me* I shouldn't live in fear of the past. You told me to face up to it and move on.'

'I did and you should.'

She was heading for her room now and he was torn between Lily in his suite and Sophia across the hall. 'Sophia, please, come back. Let's talk this through.'

'No, Jack,' she threw at him over her shoulder.

'I fell in love with you for so many reasons…'
Her voice cracked and her lashes fluttered over
her eyes as more tears escaped, each and every
one killing him. 'But being a hypocrite wasn't
one of them.'

'Sophia, please, I'm sorry. Tell me what I can
do to fix this.'

She shook her head. 'It's too late for that, Jack.'

He stepped forward again as she unlocked the
door to her room, desperate, pleading. 'Please, *I
love you.*'

She pushed the door open and turned to him.
For a second he dared to hope, dared to believe
she could give him a chance.

'I love you too, Jack…but without trust…'

She looked away, her breath shuddering through
her.

He frowned, his palms outstretched emphatically. 'I *do* trust you.'

He did. He felt that trust all the way to his
bones. He trusted her more than he had anyone
else in his life, but she wouldn't even look at him,
her body shuddering with every breath she took.

'I'm not sure you know how to trust, or how to
move on from Elena.'

She took another breath, slower this time, her
chin lifting, her eyes raking over him before coming back to meet his eyes coldly. It was admi-
rable even that she could find the strength from
somewhere.

'Goodbye, Jack. Give Lily my love. Tell her she can write to me if she likes. I'll find my own way home.'

And then she was gone, the door closing softly behind her, and he knew she meant it. That she wanted nothing more to do with him.

But she was angry, upset; she just needed time to think, time to understand how worried he'd been, why he'd said all he had. *Idiot*. He forked his hands through his hair, leaving them to hang off the back of his neck in desperation.

He should have been more controlled. He should have thought before he'd spoken. But that was just it—he'd been too upset to think.

And he'd hurt her in the process.

Really hurt her.

He turned to go back to his suite, turned again to go to Sophia, repeated the move and knew he had to go to Lily, that Sophia needed time to cool off. And that was the one thing they had—time.

All flights were grounded due to the storm.

He just hoped there was enough time to fix the damage his words had done.

CHAPTER SIXTEEN

THERE WASN'T ENOUGH TIME.

Twelve hours later and he'd learned from the hotel staff that Sophia had checked out and paid for her room. She'd left no message, no details of where she'd gone or how she planned to get home. Domestic flights were still cancelled when his own jet had been given permission to leave and so they'd travelled back to the UK without her, a fact that had Lily refusing to speak to him.

It had been nearly a week now and no word. Lily was still barely speaking to him and he couldn't concentrate on work, on anything. He'd avoided booking back into her hotel, wanting to give her the space she so obviously still needed. But it was becoming more and more obvious she wasn't coming around.

Every message, every email, every phone call, all ignored, and he couldn't bear it any longer. He had to see her. He had to explain. He had to make her see how sorry he was, how right she had been, about everything. He had been living his life in fear of the past, doing everything he'd accused her of doing.

And now he wanted a chance to show her that he *was* ready to move on. With her. If she'd have him.

He checked his watch. It was two o'clock on a Friday afternoon. She was more likely to be at work than at home and since Lily was with Ms Archer studying—something she was far more positive about now that she knew he was finding her a school—it meant he could go to see Sophia alone.

He walked into the hotel foyer and felt his heart pulsing right up through his throat. He was nervous, so nervous, and being in her space, surrounded by memories of her... He couldn't mess this up. He just couldn't.

He strode over to the reception desk and the woman behind it smiled up at him. 'Good afternoon, Mr McGregor, it's a pleasure to see you again. How may I help you?'

'I'd like to speak to Ms Lambert, if she's available.'

She frowned, her head cocking to one side as she looked to her computer screen. 'I do believe Ms Lambert is currently on leave. Let me just check...'

She navigated the system as he drummed his fingers on the countertop, hoping that she was wrong.

'Yes, I'm afraid she is away, but—'

'Mr McGregor, how lovely to see you back here.'

He turned at the familiar male voice and saw the assistant manager approaching.

'Andrew, isn't it?'

'Yes, well remembered, sir.'

Jack looked to him with hope. 'You wouldn't happen to know where I can reach Soph— Ms Lambert?'

Andrew's eyes sparkled over his faux pas. Just how much did this man know of him and Sophia? And if he did know, would he still help?

'Come this way, sir.'

He touched Jack's arm lightly and led him off to one side, out of earshot. 'I believe she's in Hertfordshire.'

'Hertfordshire?'

'Visiting her parents.'

'Her parents?'

'Yes. It seems she decided that it was time she spent some quality time with them.'

'She did?'

Andrew's eyes sparkled even more, his lips curving into a smile. 'I believe you have something to do with that.'

'I did?' Jack's own lips quirked up; he'd got something right then. 'Yes, I guess I did.'

'And since she's been there a few days already, it must be going well, don't you think?'

He did think. He really did. But it didn't change the fact that he needed to see her, he needed to put things right between them.

'I did get a message from her confirming that she would be back at work on Monday. I think she intends to travel back this evening, taking the weekend to get sorted out, that sort of thing.'

'She'll be home tonight?'

'Indeed.' He grinned now, his face so full of encouragement Jack had the sudden urge to kiss the man. Instead, he gripped his arms and thanked him.

The old man nodded, his eyes starting to glisten. 'I reckon if you try about eight-ish, she'll be home.'

'Good. Good. Thank you, Andrew. Thank you.' He started to leave.

'You're welcome…and sir?'

Jack paused midstride.

'Good luck!'

Sophia slotted the key in her lock and winced as her shoulder twinged, her body protesting after four nights in her childhood bed. But it had been worth every broken spring, every minute of lost sleep, to have reclaimed what she'd lost all these years: a place in her family home with parents who clearly loved her and had missed her so much.

How she had been blind to it before she didn't know, but it had taken Jack—*Jack*. She closed her eyes over the pain that tore through her, the ache of loss as acute as any grief, and tried to push past it. Though it was no use. She missed him. She missed him so much it hurt like a physical pain no medication could cure.

She opened her eyes and dragged in a breath as she pushed open her door and lifted her suitcase off the floor. A hot bath would help; it wouldn't stop thoughts of him, but it would ease her aching—

'Sophia?'

She froze, the voice, the man who had plagued her day and night was so real, so very real.

'Sophia?'

She turned towards it and there he was, standing in the hallway. 'How did you—?'

'Samantha let me wait for you with her and Noah.'

She nodded dumbly. So that was where he'd come from. But it didn't change things… It didn't change the fact that she couldn't be with him.

'Why are you here, Jack?'

He walked towards her. 'Can I come in?'

She dragged in more air, her eyes watering as her mind waged war on her body. One saying yes. The other saying no.

'Please, Sophia, just give me five minutes?' he pleaded, his brow raised, eyes emphatic. 'That's all I need.'

She couldn't fight him. She didn't have the

strength for it. She'd played out so many scenarios in her head and none of them could match the reality, the force of her own reaction to him, her need for him to hold her and tell her all would be okay in spite of how much he had hurt her.

'Five minutes, Jack.'

She turned away and headed to the kitchen, leaving her case in the inner hall.

She heard him close the door, his footsteps closing in behind her. He was really here. A week apart and he was now here, in her home. She remembered the last time they had been here, her eyes flitting to the sofa that had been extended out that night. The night they'd… She pressed her shaky fingers to her lips, swallowing back the sob that threatened.

'Look at me, Sophia…*please.*'

He sounded so broken, so strained, his vulnerability impossible for her to ignore as she did as he asked.

'I've missed you so much.' It rushed out on his breath, his eyes glistening with sincerity. 'I am so sorry for everything I did, everything I said. The truth is you were right. I was a hypocrite; I was living in the past, scared of it, scared of everything I couldn't control.'

He stepped closer, so close she could smell his scent, his painfully familiar cologne, and it made her body warm, her throat close over with another wave of tears, of longing, of what she daren't hope for but did anyway.

'It wasn't about my trust in you; it was about my fear of losing Lily, of losing—'

'I would have protected Lily with my life,' she forced out, hating that he could doubt it. 'I never would have put her in danger.'

'I know that, and that's what I'm saying. I trust you to keep her safe, but that day, that morning, I was so scared, not just about losing her, but you too. If anything had happened to *either* of you, I don't know how I'd cope.'

Words failed her. She could only stare at him as he continued. 'Don't you see, Sophia, you are as much a part of me as Lily is? Don't you see that's why I felt guilty about Elena? Knowing that you could become a part of me whereas she…she was Lily's mother, she was my best friend, but she was never the woman I wanted to marry, to make a life with, to make a home with.'

His words teased at her heart, every one of them pushing out the chill and replacing it with the warming beam of hope.

'I do love you, Sophia, more than I ever thought possible. I want to be with you. I want to make a life with you, here in London, or anywhere you want to go, just so long as you are with me. With us.'

He reached out to gently raise her chin, to hold her eye. '*Please* believe me.'

'I do believe you love me,' she whispered. 'But I need you to trust me too.'

'I do…and I'll prove it to you. I can be better. I try to control everything that happens to Lily, who she's exposed to, what she does… Everything. But I'm trying to change. I've promised her she can go to school. I've promised her we're going to have a home. I've promised that I'm going to try and bring you home too.'

She smiled at that. It was small, watery, but it was there.

'You've changed so much since I met you.' He curved his hand around the back of her neck, his touch lighting up the skin beneath and feeding her with his warmth. 'You've faced up to the past, your fears, you've returned to your family—'

She frowned. 'How did you know?'

'Andrew.'

She gave a gentle scoff. 'Figures.'

'Don't be mad with him. I think he knew a desperate, lovesick man when he saw me.'

She laughed softly, her eyes searching his. 'Lovesick?'

'Heartbroken. I'm nothing without you, Sophia.'

Seeing the tears in his eyes tore her apart inside but she was struggling for words, struggling to be rational when all she wanted to do was cave in to the emotions within and kiss him, hug him to her and never let him go. But how could she trust him to trust her?

'You changed with my help,' he said into her pained silence. 'Please credit me with the same ability, please help to make me a better man too.'

He was right, so right. If she could change so much, why couldn't he? She talked about his lack of trust in her, but she needed to put her faith in him too. To believe he could change. That together they could be so much better.

She couldn't hold back anymore. She launched herself at him, her lips claiming his as they parted on a surprised rush of air.

'Does that mean you will?' he tried to say against her lips that were pressed tightly to his. 'You'll give me—*us*—a chance?'

She laughed as she kissed him more. 'Yes,' she blurted. 'Yes.' She kissed him again. 'Yes.'

And this time she deepened the kiss, coaxing his whole body to life as he kissed her back, his arms folding around her and lifting her off the ground. She'd never felt so light, so free, so happy and complete.

She lifted her head, gazing down into his eyes that were so wet and so happy at once. 'I love you, Jack.'

He beamed up at her. 'I love you too, Sophia.'

'Always and for ever.'

'Are you getting all romantic and hopeful on me?'

'Yes.'

He swung her around in the kitchen and nearly

took out the pots on the drainer. 'Lily's going to be made up; she's already insisted on being a bridesmaid.'

Sophia froze, her heart pulsing in her chest. 'Are you asking me to marry you?'

'Not right now, of course. I'll prove myself to you first, but when I said all that stuff about making a life together, about you being the woman I want to marry, that's kind of where I was heading…'

She started to laugh. She couldn't help it, his boyish, almost coy expression doing her in. 'In that case, just so you know, it would be yes. Not now, of course, but when you feel ready.'

'When I feel ready?'

She nodded, making an agreeing squeak.

'Are you mocking me, Ms Lambert?'

'I wouldn't dare.'

'Why you…' And then he was tickling her and she was running away, stumbling through the living room as she tried to avoid his wandering hands, the backs of her knees colliding with the sofa, and then she was tumbling over it, taking him with her. Two bodies, all legs and arms entwined.

'Sophia?'

She wrapped her arms around his neck as she gazed up into his flushed face. 'Yes?'

'Shall we get the bed out?'

'I've a better idea. Why don't we actually christen my bed this time?'

He laughed as he kissed her. 'I'm not sure I want to waste another second. A week's been long enough.'

'True...but now we have the rest of our lives together.'

'I love the sound of that,' he murmured against her lips.

'And I love you, Jack...'

She sealed her declaration with a kiss, one that spoke of her love, her trust, her faith in their long and happy future together...and they did get to the bedroom, just much, much later.

EPILOGUE

Two years later

NEVER BEFORE HAD Jack suffered such noise. His eardrums were ringing with it. Laughter, shouting, music playing—it was about all he could do to still smile.

'You know next time Lily asks for a birthday party at home,' he grumbled in Sophia's ear, 'I'm going to suggest Iceland all over again…maybe even the North Pole. I bet it's super-quiet this time of year with Santa on holiday.'

'You said that last year.'

'Yes, well, I clearly forgot what a terrible idea this was. At least Noah only had a handful of friends at his…' He looked over the many, many heads in the room. 'I'm sure she's invited every child she's ever met, plus her entire class at school.'

Sophia merely smiled. 'She's making up for lost time, and don't forget, you did agree to her having thirty.'

'Thirty! I'm sure I didn't.'

She looked up at him. 'You were a little distracted at the time.'

Eddie chose that moment to gurgle in his mother's arms and Sophia gently bobbed him up and down.

'Now I remember, Lily asked me the day we came home with this little bundle.'

'Yes, she's not daft, that one.'

'No, but her dad clearly is.'

Sophia laughed as the doorbell sounded. 'Oh, that'll be Isla and the family. You go and get it and I'll pass Eddie to Mum.'

'Oh, no, you won't,' Samantha said, coming up beside them. 'Your mum has filled her cuddle quota; it's my turn.'

'Are you getting broody again?' Sophia grinned at her friend as she eased Eddie into her arms.

'Good heavens, no. I like to cuddle and go. It's always best when you can hand them back.'

'Amen to that,' Jack said, wincing as a high-pitched squeal bounced off the walls of their Georgian dining room.

'Jack!'

'I'm just kidding, love.'

'Get the door before they scarper at the racket. It's time to get some games going before things get out of hand.'

'Out of hand?' he said, his brows raised as his

eyes swept over the room. 'I think it's a bit late for that.'

She elbowed him. 'Quit the ribbing and get the door. Musical chairs will have them contained and entertained in one.'

'Musical what?'

'You'll see.'

'You do know how much those chairs cost, don't you?'

'Almost as much as it cost to have the room renovated, yes. Just relax, Jack, live a little.'

'I'll relax when we have our house to ourselves again.'

But in truth he wore the silliest of grins, because life couldn't be better. He had a happy daughter, a healthy son, a wife he adored and an extended family he'd never thought possible.

He made for the door and halted, swinging back to pull his wife into his arms. 'I love you, Mrs McGregor.'

Her eyes shone up at him. 'And I love you too… even when you're a grump.'

'Ouch.'

'Now, go and get Isla before they run—or, worse, freeze on our doorstep.'

He did as she bade, answering the door to Elena's mum, husband and three children. There would always be a part of him that bore regrets. The biggest one of all that Elena never got to be reunited with Isla, not properly.

But in his heart he knew she'd be happy for what their daughter now had. The one thing they'd grown up wanting and always thought unreachable.

A real family, full of love, and a place to call home.

* * * * *